Romancing
the
Nephites

A Novel

Becky Paget

Printed in the United States of America
Library of Congress Catalog Card Number: 93-070860
Covenant Communications, Inc.
Romancing the Nephites
First Printing: May 1993
94 95 96 97   10 9 8 7 6 5 4 3 2
Cover Illustration by Patric Gerber
Cover Design by Roxanne Bergener
ISBN 1-55503-552-3

Covenant
Communications, Inc.

Chapter One

600 B.C.

"Ari'el . . . Ari'el . . . Ari'el," a girl's voice echoed against the narrow walls of the old Jerusalem street. The voice was barely loud enough to echo, but in the unusual silence of the empty city, it was heard.

The owner of the name heard her sister calling. "I'm hurrying!" she called back.

Ari'el, fifth daughter of the merchant Ishmael, looked down. If she pulled up her dusty robe, she could just stretch her leg over the cobblestones and reach the next red stone with the tip of her sandal. There! She made it! She searched over the pavement of red and blue stones. The next red stone was too far. She'd have to take a safe step by jumping onto a doorsill to reach it. When she looked toward the next red stone, it was nearly hidden by the beggar hunched against the wall.

"Could you please move, sir? I'm playing a game," she spoke to him. The old man lifted his ragged head and shifted slightly, hoping to be rewarded.

"Ari'el!" her sister Lotus called again, her voice bouncing down the narrow streets.

Ari'el skipped ahead five red stones before a weak cry from the beggar halted her. Reaching into her sleeve, she retraced her steps and gave the beggar her smallest pieces of silver

"A good girl you are," he mumbled.

"Ari'el!" Lotus' voice resounded impatiently.

She hopped on ten more stones before her veil slipped into the smelly water that ran down the center of the street. "Oh, no. Not again," she muttered.

"I'm coming," Ari'el echoed back. She pulled her dress all the way up to her tunic and glided over the stones, five easy ones this time, before a string of donkeys came down the middle of the tiny road. There was nothing to do but stand on a doorstep until the whole train passed by. It was part of the game. Lotus would have to wait. She looked down, gauging her next jumps. Faded blood stained many of the stones, though it showed only on the blue. It was blood shed by the power of Babylon—the blood of those who had resisted its force. Cracks ran up the walls from the foundations of the city. She kept her eyes on the red stones.

A loud wail soared up and over the wall and joined the echo. It came again and again, a sound of mourning, magnified. It was a woman's voice. It sounded like the wail of a desert animal, lonely, aching.

Jerusalem was different this year. Every other year when they came here for the Feast of Tabernacles, the city was crowded—crowded with festive pilgrims, crowded with residents. Now it was nearly empty, echoing and suffering.

But even if half the city had been carried away to Babylon, merchants still came to Jerusalem to sell. So the family of Ishmael had made their annual pilgrimage from their home in Shilom, near Beersheba at the southern border of Judea.

Others came in from the country too, carrying their tents, curious to hear the new king, Zedekiah, speak. Though he was appointed by the powerful Babylonians, he was young and popular with his crowd of friends.

Ari'el found Lotus waiting for her around the next turn. "Honestly Ari'el, can't you walk to the market like a normal person?"

"Oh, Lotus, don't be such a dry wind over a water hole."

"If we don't hurry, we won't finish shopping before it rains! Put your veil on," Lotus whispered so the passing women couldn't hear her.

"Smell it." Ari'el stuck the veil under her sister's nose.

"Ugh!" Lotus pushed it away. "Oh Ari'el, you're always getting dirty. Can't you be more careful? Now you'll have to go back to Mother. You can't go with me to the market like this. And look at your hair! Don't you *care* how you look? Walk behind me!"

"What does it matter? I'm not even a grown-up yet. I'm only eleven." She shook her long brown hair, windblown and tangled.

"Why can't you do a simple thing like keeping your veil on?" Lotus walked ahead with the newfound dignity of a girl of thirteen. It seemed to Ari'el that *Lotus'* filmy veil never got soiled.

Fortunately for Lotus the next part of the city was paved in red only—no blue stones for Ari'el to hop over, and the blood stains were hidden. Ari'el followed Lotus without difficulty to the cloth maker's market. At the largest booth Lotus ran her fingers over the fine linens from Egypt.

"These may be the last," the shopkeeper whined.

"My brothers are bringing some from Egypt soon," Lotus replied, holding her small head high.

Ari'el smiled at the shopkeeper's reaction.

"Your family is expecting a wedding and needs fine linens?" He rubbed his palms together.

"Four weddings," Ari'el replied, curious to see how greedy he would become.

She was rewarded by seeing his eyes grow as large as pomegranates. He smiled with avarice barely concealed. "Four sisters at once? How unusual."

"Five sisters," said Ari'el. His eyes grew even wider. "Four marriages," she amended. Maybe the four sons of her Uncle Lehi would marry her four older sisters this year, if the fathers decided. Uncle Lehi's oldest son, Laman, was reluctant to commit himself.

"You must buy my linen. I'll give you a good price."

Lotus nudged Ari'el.

"How much?" Ari'el asked.

He whined before articulating. "Four measures of silver."

Lotus turned away.

"You won't get any from Egypt this year," the merchant wheedled. "This is the last of the linen. You will find your brothers' camels empty when they return. Trade with Egypt has been cut off because of the wars with Babylon."

Lotus came back. He could be right. "One measure of silver," she whispered.

"What?" the shopkeeper said.

"She said one measure of silver," Ari'el told him.

He looked at her in outrage. "That's robbery!" he roared. But Ari'el had already turned away.

"What is that commotion over there?" she asked Lotus.

The girls stared toward the city gate through a string of tall, lumbering camels. They saw laden asses, people shopping, sellers hawking wares, crowds of men waving their arms wildly as they spoke. For a nearly empty city, the market seemed very crowded. Such noise!

The shopkeeper answered Ari'el's question. "Oh, it's probably just some prophet yelling about wickedness."

"I hear they are everywhere," Lotus whispered to Ari'el. "With all the commotion about the Babylonian and Egyptian wars, the men cannot stop arguing. And prophets must tell of doom,'" Lotus quoted her older brother, Harun.

"I'd like to hear a prophet of doom," Ari'el replied. "At least he might be a real one and not one of those poor temple prophets that says everything is fine. They only say what people want to hear. Come on!"

"Ari'el, come back here! Mother said that we should be back quickly! Ari'el! The clouds are gathering—it looks like rain! We must go back. Ari'el!" Her voice rose.

"Three measures," the shopkeeper shouted after the girls.

But Ari'el was running across both red and blue stones. Lotus thought Ari'el deserved to be lost in the throng for ignoring her warning, but she followed her younger sister devotedly.

"Lotus, look, it's Uncle Lehi!" Ari'el called back.

In her surprise, Lotus forgot to be angry at Ari'el. "Uncle Lehi!" She stopped by her sister's side. "Father said Uncle Lehi has been behaving strangely lately and that he has been having dreams from God. Remember the other night when he and Father talked late into the night? They argued. I don't know who was right, but for our own uncle to preach his ideas in front of all these people . . . a man of his standing? How embarrassing! Oh let's leave before we're noticed too." She drew her veil across her face.

"Lotus, how can you say that? See what a fearless leader Uncle Lehi is, standing before the people. Perhaps they've never seen anyone like him. Imagine, a rich merchant turned prophet! They must be shocked." Ari'el smiled. Uncle Lehi was her father's business partner.

The girls stayed and listened, captivated, as Lehi told of a vision that he had of God and heaven . . . of its glories. He told of the goodness and love of God, of his mercy for the repentant sinner, of his arms forever outstretched waiting for all his children, of the Lord's love for each of them. Lehi's words had healing in them, hope and promise.

Lotus seemed to forget her embarrassment, and neither of them noticed the darkening sky as it threatened rain. Even the crowd of shoppers stopped and listened in fascination to Lehi's humble story and his pleading with the people to turn away from evil.

Ari'el's heart stirred within her with a feeling like a kindled fire. In all her life she had never felt so moved. She touched her sister on the arm. "Isn't he wonderful? He speaks the truth. Aren't you proud of him? Oh, I love Uncle Lehi!" Ari'el was not one to cry easily, but tears were streaming down her face.

"You think his words are true?"

"Of course! Uncle Lehi never lies. Lotus, I feel it right here." She laid her hand over her heart.

Suddenly, the clouds broke loose like torn goatskin bags. The listeners scurried around like splashes to find cover under the shop canopies.

"Look Lotus, there's Cousin Nephi holding a large skin over his head. He must have come with his father. Maybe we can both squeeze under it too. Come on! We haven't seen him since he left with his brothers on the caravan to Sidon. He must have just returned." Nephi was the youngest son of Uncle Lehi, nearest to Lotus and Ari'el in age.

"No! No, Ari'el!" This time Lotus grabbed the end of Ari'el's long sleeve and pulled her under the cover of a pottery vendor as Lehi continued to preach to the dwindling crowd. Rain trickled down Lehi's weather-wrinkled face.

Ari'el looked at her sister in shock. "Why won't you stand by cousin Nephi?"

"I don't want to." She wiped her fingers, dusty from Ari'el's soiled sleeve.

"But why?" Ari'el could not imagine. They had played with him all their lives.

Lotus toyed with the fringe on the tip of her veil. "I don't have to answer all your questions."

"Yes you do. That's what older sisters are for," Ari'el teased. "How can you be shy around Nephi?"

"I am afraid of him!" A sob muffled her last word and Lotus covered her face with her hands and turned away.

Ari'el couldn't believe it. "But Lotus, why? I am so sorry I upset you, Lotus. Don't cry!" She looked over at Nephi and put her arm around her sister's shoulder, totally unaware of the dirt her sleeve was leaving on Lotus' immaculate robe.

Nephi continued to stand with a few others in the center of the market, listening earnestly to his father pleading with the crowd.

"You know Mother says I'll marry him," Lotus whispered. "You know she thinks it's a sign of God's will that the number and order of the births of the girls and boys in the two families match so well. Or it did until she had you. But that didn't stop her from planning! And our brothers have already married Lehi's daughters, so her plan is partially accomplished. All that's left is to marry her four daughters to her brother's four sons. And I'm sure that idea doesn't please Nephi. He stares at me so sternly. It makes my tongue stiff."

"Oh, Lotus. Nephi couldn't ask for a better, kinder wife. But maybe the marriage won't happen anyway."

"Mother says it will."

"*Father* said the only reason Mother says that is because her necklace has only two pieces of silver on it for two sons. So she has to have something to brag about to the other women."

"I wouldn't underestimate Mother."

Ari'el watched Nephi, whose shoulders now stood taller than any man in the market. He strained forward to listen to each word his father spoke. He wore a traditional striped coat like Lehi's. Under his turban, his hair was dark and curling like Ari'el's own. He had the beginnings of a beard if one looked closely. All Ari'el's older sisters agreed that Laman, the oldest brother, was the most handsome, but Ari'el felt Nephi had a better countenance—strong, warm like a fire. Her heart warmed also as she watched him standing alone on the wet pavement. Nephi's sandals were muddy. Ari'el didn't mind, but Lotus didn't like mud.

Six summers ago when they were both in the country, Nephi had become her favorite cousin. Ari'el's family lived inside the town of Shilom and Nephi lived only a few miles away on his father's land, so they often spent time together. One day Ari'el had fallen into a hole—the entrance to a cave actually. It was dark, cold, and dusty.

Usually little Ari'el didn't show her fear of anything. How *could* she with a name like Ari'el? She had to live up to the meaning of her name, "Lioness of God." A lioness was brave and bold and loyal. But in the dark cave, her courage dwindled. She couldn't climb out, so she wept and prayed to the Lord.

Then Nephi appeared. He crawled into the dirty cave and helped her out. With his own cloak, he wiped the dust from her face, then sat her on his lap until her tears stopped. He didn't laugh at her or tell his brothers that she cried. He called her his brave little cousin and told her to keep the cave a secret. If she would never tell about the cave, he said that he would never tell she was not brave. He covered up the hole with a rock so she would never fall into it again.

After that Ari'el loved her Cousin Nephi best of all the boys she knew—even better than her own older brothers. She followed him everywhere whenever the families were together. When he studied, her shadow was over his board. When he harvested, her basket was beside his.

Ari'el couldn't understand how Lotus could be shy of Nephi. Lotus wasn't shy with the rest of the family. Ari'el wondered if maybe the possibility of marriage made a person different.

"Lotus, really. Nephi is the kindest boy there is. And there is no more obedient young man in all of Israel. You know that. You admire that. Look at him! What girl wouldn't be proud to marry him? I would! He's good and clever and dresses well—even though some girls like plain robes from Egypt better than the ones he wears. You ought to be grateful that you have a cousin like him." Ari'el's intense loyalty for Nephi showed in every word.

"I try to convince myself of that all the time," Lotus responded. "But I'm still afraid. I know he's kind to you, but when he speaks, he scares me. And he is so tall! I think I will look like a little mouse beside him. Now that we are older, and Mother is talking about betrothals, I can't even talk when I'm near him."

"You have to be strong, Lotus! He will take good care of you. I know. Be glad you aren't like me, the extra girl who has no cousin to marry. Who will marry me when I grow up? So many young men in Jerusalem were carried off to Babylon and so few of those left are righteous. There are even fewer at home in Shilom."

Ari'el said all those things for Lotus' benefit, without bitterness. She was too young and naive to realize that she could no longer follow Nephi when he married. No thought of romance for herself touched her mind. In contrast to Ari'el, concern about betrothals filled nearly every waking moment of Lotus' days. To be unaffected by romance was one of the few ways for Ari'el to enjoy some small individuality among her sisters. For Ari'el, men and boys were merely people to have fun with, people with whom she could do the things her sisters would never dare. She did not think of them as potential husbands. She never even considered such a thing!

"Oh, Ari'el, someday you'll really care about having a husband." Lotus turned, suddenly concerned. "When the time comes that you do, Father will find you one somehow. Why, look how pretty you could be. Lean over and see yourself in this puddle. If your hair was oiled and combed and your veil washed, you could be even finer looking than our sister Zenobia—but don't tell *her* that!"

Ari'el looked at her reflection and wiggled her eyebrows up and down. She saw unruly hair and pale skin. Well, pale skin would be good if the day ever came that she needed to attract a man. However, once she got home and went out in the spring sunshine again, she would become as brown as a nut. A dimple appeared as she smiled. She touched it with a muddy finger.

The two girls smiled at their reflections in the water until a donkey stepped into the other end of the puddle and scattered their reflections. "Oh, Lotus, how silly you are!" Ari'el laughed and Lotus joined her. She might grow prettier than Lotus, but she would never be as beautiful as Zenobia! The cedars of Lebanon would fall! Lotus talked so foolishly today.

While the girls were speaking, Lehi's voice rose in volume, calling out the judgements of God, prophesying the destruction of Jerusalem by the Babylonians, and they began listening again. He begged the people to turn back to their God, to stop oppressing the poor, to stop striving after the pride of Egypt, to stop worshiping heathen gods. He pled with them to cleanse the temple from evil, to save themselves from destruction. They were already paying the consequences of their sins. Hadn't the rich and important people and the treasures of the temple been carried away? If the people didn't repent, surely the whole city would be destroyed. Now was the time to repent.

The people under the crowded canopies began to talk loudly about what Lehi was saying. "Blasphemy!" yelled a brash young man from the other side of the market who wore the popular fashions of Egypt. He smiled at his friends, who obviously followed the same fad he did, then threw a stone at Lehi.

A fat woman standing near Ari'el and Lotus shook at such impudence. She waved her arm at the young man. "Imagine, throwing a stone at an elder! Your father ought to be told, young man," she called.

But the irreverent youth only laughed and called Lehi a crazy, old prophet. His friends laughed with him.

"So what if you're a rich, important merchant? You've gone crazy!" they shouted to Lehi, then began throwing more stones, although the young men were too far from Lehi to make their mark.

Ari'el could see that Nephi's knuckles were clenched tightly on the wet sheepskin, ready to jump to his father's defense if he needed help. He didn't notice his two young cousins.

Lotus and Ari'el moved further back under the canopy, away from the flying stones. A group of men dressed in great finery had gathered near them—obviously royalty of Israel. Ari'el stared at their imported silk robes with tassels hanging from embroidered edges. Elegant turbans crowned their curled grey hair. The girls heard one of them murmuring.

"Lehi's turned traitor. He cannot be allowed to get away with this. He'll stir up antinationalist feelings. The people and the armies must not sympathize with Babylon. Look what they've done to us, those Babylonian dogs! When the time is ripe to rise again against Babylon, Neco of Egypt will be behind us. Lehi must be silenced!"

Lotus grabbed Ari'el's hand with trembling fingers. The two girls were so frightened that they nearly stopped breathing. Ari'el's fingers began to fidget too. These men were threatening her Uncle Lehi. She tried to steady her breath and stand normally.

A man with many coats replied, "I never thought Lehi, of all men, would turn toward Babylon. Submission indeed! And who is he to talk about repentance? We don't need to repent!" The man spat in the street. "That is what I think of Lehi's 'prophesies'! No king of Babylon shall rule the people of the Lord! We will rule ourselves!"

The spittle splashed on the hem of Ari'el's dress. Ari'el glared at the men, who had turned away from Uncle Lehi and were now facing her direction. She stood bravely, as her Cousin Nephi would have done.

"The words Lehi says are true. He is my uncle and I am proud of him!" Ari'el proclaimed, her deep brown eyes flashing, her chin held firm. She was oddly dignified in spite of the streak of mud on her cheek.

The men stared at her earnest face, shining with sincerity. The man who had spoken started to laugh and was soon joined by the others.

"What a tigress!" one man said.

Another among the group of rulers, a young man dressed in a short military uniform, said appreciatively, "The prophet Lehi will have to look well to his household. This niece will be a spirited beauty!"

Ari'el's dark eyes fastened on him like two knives waiting to be thrown. One of the rulers looked thoughtfully at the young soldier and Ari'el.

Lotus grabbed Ari'el's arm and pulled her away from the men's roaring laughter.

"Nephi could hit that impudent soldier for me!" Ari'el cried. "Nephi is much larger than he is."

"He wouldn't do it." Lotus held Ari'el's coat sleeve tightly and kept going.

Ari'el glanced back at the scene as she was pulled toward the house they were staying in. More people threw rocks at Lehi. Still, he continued to preach—until a stone struck his head. Ari'el could bear to look no longer.

"They were right to name you Ari'el," Lotus complained. "You have more bravery than is good for you. How could you open your mouth to those men? You're more trouble than a string of hungry goats! This is the last time I take you anywhere! What will Mother say?"

"Just don't tell her. Remember, your name is Lotus, meaning the bloom of forgetfulness," Ari'el teased, even though Lotus, who did not share Ari'el's sense of humor, would not understand. That made teasing her sister even more fun. But in her heart, she worried about what the men had said and wondered if Uncle Lehi was now safe from the crowd. Was he hurt? Would the pompous leaders carry out their threats? And most importantly, had Nephi been able to rescue him from the crowd?

Chapter Two

Ari'el was glad when they left Jerusalem. She hoped her Uncle Lehi had gone home too. She had not heard of him preaching in the marketplace anymore, but because of the stones and the words of the hard-hearted men, she feared for his safety. She told her father what the finely dressed men had said, but he told her that their words were no more than groanings in the wind. She trusted her father and set the matter aside.

Shilom, with its surrounding fields of rock, earth, and flowers, was a happy place, Ari'el thought as she went out of the town to gather dry dung for her mother's cooking fire. She thought her heart would burst with light just as the sun did when it rose over Mount Lehi. Her laughter rang out across the spring meadow. She kicked up her sandal from the end of her long, thin leg and twirled around, hanging tightly to the load held in her upturned skirt. Her tongue clicked the sound of the timbrel as she glided smoothly to the right and then to the left before she ended on a twirl. There would be dancing soon. Imagine, four weddings! She glowed with happiness beyond that of the yellow sun warming her skin. Surely Laman would have to betroth her eldest sister, Yobina, this spring. After all, Yobina was nineteen and the families expected it. He could put it off no longer.

Tucking her hem into her girdle securely, Ari'el climbed the rise to the town, stopping now and then to add a twirl to her step. The massive stone walls of Shilom loomed over her head against the southern blue of the sky. Already the year was growing warm.

Her feet slowed to carry her in a more circumspect, even rhythm through the city gate and into the marketplace. Here, she knew every unchanging stone by heart and the length of each footstep it took to walk from the well to her home and from the gate to her home. Her feet could lead her to where each family lived, to where she could find a sweet treat on baking days. She could find her way in darkness and rain, or even while blindfolded. She knew where to step to avoid potholes and waste water. This town was home to Ari'el.

The guardhouse in the gate of the city was empty of its military personnel. Her father, Ishmael, said the new king, Zedekiah, would appoint his own men soon. Military changes happened often because of the change in kings, and the kings changed frequently because Judah was always ruled by one of its larger, more powerful neighbors. Even though the Jews often rebelled against this oppression, they were crushed again and again. Time after time they were defeated and a new ruler was installed.

But regardless of who ruled in Jerusalem or what military commander was in residence at Shilom, Ari'el knew that the bench along the wall of the guardhouse would always be filled with the same old men who sat and talked from morning until evening. That never changed. Ari'el bowed to them as she passed, as good manners required. She knew them well as her father's friends.

Across from the gateway stood the well, the place where women of all ages could be found. In contrast to the men, they worked as they talked.

"Ari'el, Ari'el! Come here!" Ari'el knew she could not walk past the well without giving an account of her family.

"How was Jerusalem?" Several faces turned toward her, some wrinkled, some smooth. Ari'el knew she would say nothing of Uncle Lehi and the crowd who mocked him.

She smiled at the women, who rarely traveled to Jerusalem and said merely, "Haunted and nearly empty. It's good to be home!"

"The markets, they are still fine?"

"Too noisy! I prefer Shilom."

"I suppose you would, but then you have brothers who travel to Egypt to bring you fine linens and other beautiful things." Ari'el knew that most of these women owned only one dress, a good heavy dress made to last a lifetime. Few had extra silver for finery.

"This year their camels may come back empty, according to the linen vendor in Jerusalem. But then, maybe he told us that because he wanted a good price for his linen."

The woman named Muriel stepped forward. "Linen? Then the wedding is on? I always thought Laman should have been wed to Yobina long ago. It's a disgrace."

Ari'el turned crimson, listening to common gossip regarding her family. She held her chin up as she told the woman, "I must get this fuel home to my mother."

As she walked away, Ari'el heard one woman say, "You shouldn't have said that, Muriel. Now you have offended her and she will tell her mother. It isn't wise to openly criticize the house of Lehi or Ishmael. They own our land."

"What can a child do?" Muriel scoffed.

But Ari'el wouldn't tell anyone. It would only hurt Yobina to know she was talked about.

Yobina had been talked about since she was born, which was how she, like Job, came to be called "the afflicted one." The women of the village differed in their opinions of the degree of her affliction, depending on the degree to which they shared her affliction. Yobina had grown up hopelessly homely, and was often compared to her sister, the prettiest baby ever born in Shilom. Zenobia was as beautiful as her older sister Yobina was homely, and nothing could disguise that fact. They both knew it.

Older women said Yobina was a blessing, like the virtuous woman in the proverbs of Solomon. She behaved as a model daughter for the town, talented and hardworking. These qualities, they said, made up for what she lacked in appearance. But there were always those other women with their wagging tongues, especially when Laman was so handsome and Yobina so plain.

Ari'el entered the door in the wall around their home, dropped her load in the open courtyard beside the fire pit, and crossed the threshold of the inside room reserved for women. She heard the beautiful Zenobia saying, "I love the way babies fit right in your arms—so small, yet so whole. I love their tiny hands and feet and the way their little eyelashes lay against their cheeks while they sleep. They're so darling! I want my own baby! My own!"

"Would you like to have my job this summer, watching the children and the lambs?" Ari'el offered.

"At my age? Hah! Anyway, who likes the little *children*? They're all brats. I said *babies*. Little, sweet babies that coo and gurgle. I want my own baby, my very own. After all, I'm seventeen. I'm a woman now!" Zenobia said.

Indeed, she looked like a woman, the kind of woman men turned to look at as often as women turned to look at beautiful babies. Zenobia was naturally aware of her appeal and made good use of the popular styles of Egypt. Her father, who could afford to indulge her pleas for thin, sheer linen, would grow weary of her pleading and grant her requests. Zenobia loved the way the soft fabric clung to her body. No other girl in Shilom owned dresses of such fabric except her sister, Isis, who had been born just after Zenobia. But somehow the thin linen didn't do for Isis what it did for Zenobia.

To make up for what she lacked in natural beauty, Isis adorned her ears, nose, and neck—and her ankles and wrists—with jewelry. She tinkled like a trader. One could always hear Isis coming, not only by the jingling of her jewelry but by her giggles, which Ari'el heard now while Isis and her sisters speculated on Laman's expected visit of betrothal.

"Did you hear if Laman is home yet?" Lotus asked. "He'll soon come calling on Yobina with a camel full of betrothal gifts."

"Not yet. I wonder why he is so late?"

"Laman probably doesn't want to marry Yobina, and he is stalling for time," Isis giggled to Zenobia.

Yobina quietly leaned over and stuck Isis with her weaving needle.

"Ouch!" Isis jumped, then whirled around, her mouth open wide. "She stuck me!"

"Yobina!" Lotus and Ari'el said together. Yobina had gone back to her weaving, fingers shaking. Her sisters knew Yobina's gentle nature. That she would do something so unkind showed how deeply Laman's tardiness hurt her.

Isis recovered quickly. "I meant every word! When you were a child, Laman used to call you 'sheep face.' Lemuel used to *baa* at you whenever you came near him."

"Isis," Lotus whispered in warning. She noticed Yobina's lips were trembling.

"I don't care what they called me," Yobina said in her soft voice.

Zenobia retorted, "You ought to! None of us can get married until you do!"

15

Pushed this far, Yobina's composure finally slipped. "So what if I am 'sheep faced!'" she shouted. "There are worse things!"

"Like what?" Zenobia and Isis smirked.

"Like being disobedient and rebellious. At least I do what I'm told and don't sneak around behind Mother's back. And I don't dress like an Egyptian water wader. And I don't say things that hurt other people. And I can weave! I'm the best weaver in Shilom."

Zenobia smoothly adjusted her embroidered girdle across her slim waist. "You think that counts with a man like Laman? Laman likes *beautiful* women . . . like me. He could hire ten good weavers if he needed them." Zenobia paused then said deliberately, "Laman kissed me. *Me!* It's me he wants, not Yobina!"

That was the final insult. Yobina put her head down against the loom. Great gasps came from her. Ari'el laid her hand on Yobina's shoulder and glared at her beautiful sister. "You stop that," she said and then to Yobina she whispered, "He's not worth it."

Lotus spoke next. "Zenobia! How could you do such a thing? What would Lemuel think? You're to marry him, not Laman."

"Who cares about Lemuel?" Zenobia said carelessly as she adjusted the comb in her hair. "And Yobina needed to know the truth."

"But to let a man . . . " Lotus turned red and couldn't finish the sentence.

"You better not tell Mother."

Ari'el stroked Yobina's hair. It was true that Laman did not admire her. How hard it would be to marry a man that didn't admire you . . . or love you! And how humiliating if he made you wait so long. Maybe she herself was fortunate she had no cousin to marry, no man at all to make her wait or wonder if he would want her.

And Zenobia had kissed Laman! Ari'el wondered what it would be like to kiss a man . . . it would be like kissing a hairy goat! Why had Laman kissed Zenobia? Of course, nothing was official. Laman had never spoken to Father of a marriage to Yobina as far as they knew. But Mother always said Laman would marry Yobina, Lemuel would marry Zenobia, Sam would marry Isis, and Nephi would marry Lotus. It was the fondest wish of Mother's heart. She and Aunt Sariah had planned the marriages as each of their children had been born. Mother always said it was God's will that these children marry each other.

"I should be the one to marry Laman," Zenobia said. "What perfectly exquisite babies we would have!"

"But you should marry Lemuel," Lotus protested. "He is the second son and you are the second daughter. Mother named you after the Queen of Sheba because Lemuel is another name for King Solomon. And you're beautiful like the ancient Zenobia. Mother meant for the two of you to be a matched pair."

"Well, Solomon and the ancient Zenobia may have admired each other for their wit and wisdom, but they never married."

Zenobia did have a point.

"I like Lemuel. He always makes me laugh," Isis defended him. "I like him much better than Sam. How would you like to be me and have to marry Sam? His children will grow up thinking they are deaf because they will never hear a word spoken to them. I'll think I'm deaf, too." She giggled.

Ari'el thought of Sam. He was Lehi's third son, as Isis was Ishmael's third daughter. True, he seldom spoke, but he had such a tender smile, like a new spring flower. Ari'el had always liked him. Besides, he was a loyal friend to Nephi, which was Sam's best feature in Ari'el's eyes. But still, even if he didn't talk much, Sam communicated. It took time and patience to learn his ways, but if you watched him long enough, you could know his thoughts.

Perhaps it was his silence that kept Sam away from the trouble-makers. Sam never ran through the hills with the wild boys, and they didn't bother with him. He was like a large rock in the desert, solid and immovable in his loyalty. He would make a good husband.

"I like Sam," Lotus said. "I understand him."

"You would," Isis said. "He's a model child—just like you."

Zenobia stretched her legs. "I'm not complaining. I know Lemuel is no fatted calf, but he'll be rich enough. They all will be. It's just that Laman is the firstborn." Laman would be the richest someday. That made him doubly desirable.

"If Yobina doesn't mind my saying so," Isis looked toward Yobina's still bent head, "I think Laman ought to marry both you and Yobina."

Ari'el protested. "Isis! You know Uncle Lehi doesn't believe in men having more than one wife!"

"Lizard spit! Almost every rich man we know has several wives. And Laman will be so rich when he receives his inheritance he could marry all of us!"

Zenobia looked at Isis. "Ari'el is right about Uncle Lehi. He would never agree. The best solution is to find another man for Yobina." She added in a whisper, "Some man who wants a *weaver*!"

Isis giggled as Zenobia had intended her to do.

Lotus crossed the room to fetch more grain to grind. "How can you talk so? Besides being cruel, you know that no matter what we say, this is a serious matter that only Father can decide."

"Lotus, if God waited for Adam to decide, the human race would never be. Eve took matters into her own hands. She was the one to eat the fruit."

Lotus was shocked into stillness.

Isis rolled on a mat laughing. "Oh, Zenobia, you're so funny! If God had waited for Adam . . . !"

"It *was* rather clever." Zenobia was clearly proud of herself.

"I know what would work!" Isis sat up suddenly. "Maybe some old man, a rich old man, would like a younger wife like Yobina!"

"Oh, Isis," Ari'el said. She was sick of Isis' foolish ideas. Her mind was like a water pot with holes in it.

Zenobia stopped arranging her braids. "I have a better idea. We can make her look rich. I know . . . we could dress her in the wedding veils of Amber and Almira! Can't you see her walking through the market, in all her splendor?"

Yobina crept out of the room. She'd had more than enough insults for one day.

"How I would like those wedding veils," Zenobia continued with sudden passion. "They have more silver sewn on them than any from Gaza to Beersheba!" Amber and Almira had married Ishmael's sons, Harun and Quarun. As the daughters of wealthy Uncle Lehi, the two sisters had brought generous dowries to their husbands.

"Don't set your hearts on riches," Lotus warned. Lotus never dressed in a way to call attention to herself. "The linen vendor in Jerusalem said that trade with Egypt was cut off."

Isis interrupted. "No goods from Egypt! That's horrid! Harun promised me a wide necklace like he gave Amber. I'll just die if I have to wear my old chains this year. How can I get my hair to stay without my oil? And what would I do without my skin cream!"'

"You could *wrinkle*," said Ari'el, exasperated.

Zenobia said, "The point is, we may be poor. All the more reason to work on a man for Yobina. I'm seventeen! I am too old to wait much longer!" She clenched her hands together in front of her.

"Oh Zenobia, you're not old," said Lotus.

"Just wait until *you're* seventeen. Hah! Unfulfilled dreams. When you are only thirteen, you think you have years to be married and so many prospective husbands. I did. Then all those young men got carried off. I should have done something about it a long time ago! At least I would have a baby by now." With that, Zenobia headed to the door.

Isis asked, "Where are you going?"

"To the guardhouse. I want to look over the new soldiers. At least they are men," said Zenobia.

Isis giggled. "Let's go!"

Lotus cried, "Zenobia, Isis! You mustn't."

Zenobia faced Lotus, "And don't tell Mother, or I won't let you borrow my new veil this Sabbath!"

They went out after a good deal of preening before the brass pot.

Suddenly Ari'el laughed. "Let them go. All they will find is old men. The guardhouse is empty."

Chapter Three

"Where is Uncle Lehi?" Ari'el's nephew asked. Ari'el called him "Big Ears" for more reasons than the obvious one. He was the son of her oldest brother Harun. Ari'el often watched four of her brothers' children—a job she was doing that afternoon.

Ari'el's nieces and nephews loved Uncle Lehi's stories as much as she did, and she did not know why Uncle Lehi had not come to see them. She hoped that the trading journey of Lehi's family was more prosperous than that of her brothers, who had recently returned from Egypt, their camels empty. Babylon had cut off the trade just as the linen seller in Jerusalem predicted. But Lehi's sons had gone to trade in the seaport of Sidon.

"Do you think the Babylonians came back and carried them away?" said Big Ears.

Ari'el gasped. What a terrible thought! "I hope not."

"Do you think Lemuel got in trouble again?"

"What do you know about that?" Ari'el asked sharply.

"I heard my father talking about Lemuel. When he was little, a group of his friends went over the mountain and scared a flock of sheep. The only person watching the sheep was a deaf old shepherd. So all the sheep ran away from him and were scattered all over the mountain." He laughed.

Ari'el gasped a second time. "I hope you don't think that was funny! You don't want to follow Lemuel's bad example and do things that hurt other people. Besides, I heard that Lemuel and his friends got caught and had to find all the sheep themselves. Served them right."

"Father laughed because some sheep got mixed up in another flock and the owners wouldn't give them back. The real owners got so mad at them that they haven't spoken to each other for seven years." Big Ears laughed again unrepentantly.

"It reopened a three-hundred-year feud. I don't think that's funny and you shouldn't either."

"My father does!"

"Harun wouldn't think it was funny if he knew you heard. And Uncle Lehi made Lemuel pay for every sheep they lost. Was Lemuel mad!"

"Oh." Big Ears twirled a stick around for a moment. "You think Lemuel is bad, don't you?"

Ari'el bit her lower lip. "No, he used to do some very irresponsible things, but he's grown up now. He's twenty." Still, not too long ago Lemuel had taken a drink of water from the well of an unfriendly tribe when he was on a caravan trip. His father had to give up their whole load of goods to save Lemuel's life. Ari'el didn't need to tell Big Ears *that* story. At least Lemuel seemed to settle down after that incident.

Lemuel looked up to his brother Laman, did anything he said, and tried to be like him. Still, Lemuel was friendlier than Laman, who had a mean streak in him. Laman was far too clever to be caught in any wickedness. But when Lemuel followed Laman, he was always caught—every time. So Lemuel was considered the bad son. But Ari'el knew better. Laman was like a dark Jerusalem alley at night.

And he was proud, dressing like a prince and never bothering to talk to Ari'el or the younger children. She felt like a little fly buzzing around him ready to be swatted. Of course, he was a lot older than her, older than all of them—especially Sam, Nephi, Lotus, and herself. He was older than her big sisters and his two married sisters as well. Maybe that was why he ignored her. Maybe when they were all grown-ups he would be different. The only girls in the family he ever paid attention to were Zenobia and Isis because they were pretty. And he kissed Zenobia. Imagine! The great Laman kissing Zenobia . . .

"What did you say, Ari'el?"

"Oh!" She looked at Big Ears. Good thing he couldn't read her thoughts! "Why don't we all play beside the big rocks, the ones we named Sheba."

"The ones Aunt Zenobia named?"

"Yes."

"Last one there is a dog!" he yelled and ran off down the slope. The lambs scrambled after, then Ari'el and the other children followed with a surprising renewal of energy. Ari'el picked up two slow lambs. With the lunch tied up in her skirt, she followed the path trampled by children's footsteps.

When they reached the spot, Ari'el lay back on the damp spring earth soaking up tender rays of sun while the children frolicked with the fuzzy new lambs. Small children made nice sounds, sounds impervious to adult problems, politics, gossip, and poverty. She felt such peace when she was with the children. And to think she would have a whole summer of it! It was heaven!

Ari'el couldn't lie still very long. There were too many places to see—the flat fishing rock; Methuselah, the oldest olive tree all twisted, grey, and wrinkled; and the stone fortress the small boys of the town built so they could play soldiers.

The creek flowing through the usually dry wadi, or stream bed, was swollen with rains that fell on Mount Lehi, which towered over Uncle Lehi's lands to the east of Shilom. Lehi's family didn't live in town; rather they had a fortified home up the hill in the middle of his land. Their home was grand, with many beautifully furnished rooms, and they had many servants.

The water coming from Mount Lehi gurgled with news, nice news. At one place it said, "Maybe your cousins will come home soon." At another place it said, "Maybe they will come to visit today." Where it tumbled over two rocks it said, "Maybe they will bring you something exotic and beautiful from the seaport of Sidon this year. Maybe there will be a wedding!"

The gurgling of the brook merged with the laughter of the children and the bleating of the lambs. It reminded Ari'el of the many happy years she and Lotus had toddled after Nephi and Sam as the boys helped in the olive and grape orchards. During that time, Isis and Zenobia had charge of the girls, though for the most part, Zenobia ignored the children she was supposed to care for and left them to do whatever they pleased. It had pleased Ari'el to follow after Nephi, who had rescued her many times—from treetops, grape presses, and even Zenobia.

Now it was her turn to rescue and entertain young children. Ari'el decided it was time to offer a diversion, a game they all played when she was younger. It had been Zenobia's favorite because she could be the queen.

"Do you see that tamarisk tree over there? Let's pretend it's the palace of King Zedekiah. I'll put red blossoms in the girls' hair and the boys can make swords of sticks." Pointing to the two oldest, she said, "You can sit on the limbs and be the king and queen! I'll be a servant."

"I want to be the queen," the youngest niece wailed.

"Is that all right with you?" Ari'el asked the first queen.

"I want to be the queen. She can be my princess."

"Princess, princess, I'm going to be a princess!"

"You can be one because long ago there were princes and princesses in our family, in the Kingdom of Israel. It was long before our ancestors came to the land of Jerusalem. Your grandfather said so," Ari'el said. When he was young, Laman always claimed to be the king or the prince. Now he seemed content enough simply to dress like one.

"Who were they?" asked Big Ears, who was enjoying his role as King of the Tamarisk Tree.

"I don't know. Your grandfather doesn't know either. Our part of the family doesn't keep the records. We only know by word of mouth. Our princes were the kind that were heads of families."

The king of the tree decreed, "Lots of people are related to that kind of prince. That's not special."

"Well, Uncle Lehi said that we can all become children of the Messiah, who is our Heavenly King. That is best of all!"

"My father says Uncle Lehi's a crazy old man," the queen repeated solemnly. "Is he really a crazy old man, Ari'el?"

"Of course not! He believes in the Lord and talks to him. That's not crazy. I heard him speaking before the people of Jerusalem, just like a prophet. Everyone listened. You would have been so proud of him! And do you know what I did? I spoke up in his favor to some real live princes! Relatives of King Zedekiah!"

"Ah." They were impressed. "You must be the bravest person alive," the boys said.

Ari'el gurgled like the brook. "Lotus didn't think so. And your grandmother hit me with the broom when Lotus told her! Six times!"

"I still think it was brave," said Big Ears. "I'm going to do that when I grow up!"

By that time each girl had a bright red bloom behind her ear and the boys had positions of honor in the tree branches. The game continued with the grand feast until the sun was high in the sky, and it went on until the royal resting time in the shade of the tree palace.

If Ari'el closed her eyes, she could pretend she was playing with her cousins and sisters again. That was more fun. Nephi always had to be king because Sam never wanted to be one. He always wanted to be a camel. She remembered a time that Nephi played king when Zenobia was queen. He pushed her right out of the tree when she acted too bossy. Everyone laughed at that. Zenobia wouldn't talk to Nephi for days!

As the tree shadow grew longer she gathered up the lambs and the children, and together they headed for the town on the rise by the wadi. As the group of children approached the town gate, they saw the shepherd boy bringing the town flock home for the night. Hopping up and down to attract his attention, Ari'el yelled a greeting to him.

"Peace to you, Ari'el," the shepherd called back across his bleating flock. "So *you're* keeping the lambs and babies this year?"

"Of course," she called over the noise. He was her age, why should he be surprised? "Where have you been today?"

"Up toward the mountain. Lehi's servants say he is gone and he's not coming back."

Ari'el stood still. "What do you mean?"

"Lehi and his family. They've left Judea."

Ari'el was dumbfounded for a moment. Gathering her wits, she asked, "Where have they gone?"

"That's the whole point. Nobody knows. They disappeared completely!"

"Disappeared? The whole family?" Although they were getting closer together and she didn't have to shout, Ari'el found her voice rising.

"That's right. Disappeared." And then hurriedly he added, "I have to keep up with the flock. Good-bye, Ari'el."

"Peace be with you," she said automatically.

"Did you say they disappeared, the whole of Lehi's family?" a woman coming into town called out to him.

"That's what they say up the mountain!" said the boy, calling behind him as he struggled to keep up with his flock.

Anxious to be the first to spread the news, the woman scurried through the gate.

Ari'el could barely walk, prey to a host of emotions and memories of Lehi preaching bravely in the Jerusalem marketplace, of the faces of the angry crowd, of the words of the men behind her that day, of the rock that hit Lehi's head, of the bloodstains on the blue cobblestones, of Nephi's feet running forward. And Nephi! Her eyes might never see her beloved cousin again. Her feet might never follow him. Her ears might never hear his kind words or laughter. A sob crawled up through Ari'el's throat. What would her world be like without Nephi?

Chapter Four

"Have you heard?" Ari'el's veil was off again, her hem was muddy, and the remnants of lunch were falling out of her upturned skirt. Two skinny knees showed.

"Be still, child!" her mother, Zipporah, said. "Go, wash yourself. Fix your hair."

"But Mother!"

"Now!" Zipporah waved her robed arm in the direction of the water jar. She shook her finger and frowned when Ari'el hesitated.

Ari'el obeyed. She poured a bit of water into a basin and splashed it on her face. The cool water felt good on her face. She wouldn't cry! She wouldn't!

"Isis, Uncle Lehi and his family are gone. They've disappeared," Ari'el whispered.

Isis turned toward her. "What did you say?"

"They're gone. The shepherd was at Lehi's and the servants say he's disappeared!"

Isis shrieked long and piercingly, which surprised Ari'el. All that grief over Sam? But Isis always complained about Sam. Without thinking, Ari'el took the bowl of water and threw it on Isis to silence her hysterics. Isis' noise was reduced to a quiet sob.

The others gathered around her.

"What did you do to her?" Zenobia asked Ari'el.

"They're not coming . . . " Isis sobbed. "I won't be married!" But despite her sniffles, Ari'el thought Isis enjoyed being the center of attention.

Zenobia turned to Isis and said coldly, "Talk sensibly, Isis. What do you mean you won't be married?"

But Isis only sobbed again, which left Ari'el to explain. Although she had sworn not to weep, her voice broke as she relayed the news.

Ari'el's mother, Zipporah, exclaimed, "That can't be! Why would my brother go away? The Babylonians have left us and we have weddings planned."

Lotus interrupted. "The men in Jerusalem, Mother. They spoke against him. Perhaps . . . "

No one liked to think of the "perhaps." There was profound silence for a moment before Zipporah tore her cloak and knelt in the dust of the courtyard, crying.

"Oh, Lord God!" Zipporah said to the heavens. "You sent me only two sons! I have five daughters who must marry. What have I done to deserve this?"

Zenobia said nothing as she stared at her dreams in the dust. She felt an overpowering anger at God and then at Uncle Lehi for embroiling himself in a situation that would thwart her plans. Yobina's homely face showed conflicting feelings of relief and chagrin. Then relief won and dared to reveal itself. Lotus immediately showed open relief that she need not marry.

Suddenly Ari'el's voice was strong and clear above the mourning of Zipporah and Isis. "How can you be so concerned about weddings when Uncle Lehi's life may be in danger? You heard what Lotus said. What if she's right?"

The women of the house grew quiet and looked at her. Fear replaced relief on Lotus' face.

Zipporah stood up. "That's true, child," she said to Ari'el. She walked across the courtyard. "Your father. What will he say? What will he do? What more can happen to us? First the camels return empty and now Lehi is gone. What more can happen? They say evil comes in threes!" She threw dust on her forehead as a token of her sorrow.

"Mother, don't! Maybe it's only gossip," Yobina pleaded.

"Where's your father? Why is that man never here when he's needed? Oh, Ishmael," Zipporah began again to weep.

"Run and find Father, Ari'el," Zenobia ordered.

Ari'el was glad to escape. She retraced her steps through the narrow lane back to the market. The sky, fiery red in the west, cast long, deep shadows across the narrow streets. Ari'el crept through the tunnels of darkness between the houses. Above her, on the rooftops, dark shapes, silhouetted against red embers of sunset, were gesturing and yelling.

"Did you hear the news?"

"What do you think?"

"They say they were all murdered in their sleep and the bodies were dragged off and buried in the debtors' grave."

"No, really?"

Further down the street she heard more whispers. "They say Lehi was carried off to Babylon."

"It's all that business of him saying he was a prophet."

"Maybe King Zedekiah sent them to Egypt."

"As slaves."

With every corner Ari'el turned, someone had a different story to tell.

"They always were an odd clan. Came from somewhere up north."

"Who will inherit his fortune? They say all his sons are gone too."

"Most likely Ishmael. He's nearest of kin."

"They say they found the bodies."

"Esther says they'll be back next week."

"Who knows what to believe?"

The voices chased Ari'el down the dark street. Desperately, she ran, her only hope the light at the opening to the marketplace.

Ishmael watched his beloved daughter flying across the open square with amused tolerance. "Father, Father," she called to Ishmael across the dimly lighted marketplace as he sat with his friends, leaning against the warm brick wall of the guardhouse. To Ishmael's astonishment, Ari'el flung herself into his outstretched arms and buried her face in his long beard.

Ishmael loved his family greatly, even though there were too many females in it for comfort. Feeling his age, Ishmael nowadays preferred to let the younger generation take over for him. After all, at his age it was his due.

He smoothed Ari'el's hair. "Now, what has happened to cause my brave little girl to hug her father so tightly?" He spoke to the old men resting with him, "Such a fuss, such a fuss. Will you have such a fuss to greet you at home?"

"We don't have your problems," one man answered. "All those daughters. Tsk, tsk."

Despite her audience, Ari'el sniffled, "Father, they say terrible things about Uncle Lehi. Horrible things."

"That's only the talk of women. Pay no attention. Women must have *something* to talk about."

The row of bellies jiggled as the men chuckled their agreement.

"But it might be true!" she protested.

"Don't worry little one, put your head on your father's shoulder." He held her as if she were a child, but her long legs betrayed her age.

"She's not a little one anymore!" one of his friends joked. "Soon you will have five daughters to marry off!"

"And Ishmael says he is not worried about Lehi!" another man scoffed.

Reluctantly, Ishmael stood up with Ari'el. "It seems I must begin to worry," he sighed. Ishmael had spent many hard years traveling, trading, riding through the deserts. He and Lehi shared a prosperous business, though Ishmael's part had not been as prosperous as Lehi's. But then, the House of Lehi had been more prosperous than the House of Ishmael for several generations.

And now Lehi had disappeared. As impossible as it seemed, Lehi *had* been behaving strangely lately, telling of strange dreams and consorting with prophets—even preaching, according to his daughters. Ishmael had decided he'd have to have a talk with his brother-in-law Lehi next time he saw him.

"Mother wants you to come right away. She put dust on her face," Ari'el finally ventured.

"Women! How can one man have so many women? Solomon must have been crazy!" Ishmael muttered.

The men chuckled as Ari'el and her father crossed the empty marketplace.

Chapter Five

Zenobia turned her face away from her mother. "I won't go!"

"But Zenobia," Zipporah explained patiently, "all our lives we have been friends of the family of the bride. The family of Ishmael will go. It would bring shame on our house if we didn't attend Dinah's wedding."

"But Mother, everyone will laugh at us. I can't bear it," Isis protested. "I can't!"

Zipporah said firmly, "No one with any sense will laugh at us. Too many young men are gone from Jerusalem and too many girls are without their betrothed. Are you so unusual? Those who are our friends will sympathize and those who aren't—they won't dare laugh!"

Isis pleaded, "But Mother, it is shameful to be sixteen and not married. All the gossip about Lehi and his household going away. We were to marry them, and now they are gone. How can we bear to attend the wedding of an ugly young girl of fourteen?" Isis pleaded.

"I wasn't married until I was eighteen. And I went to every wedding. We must have patience. Your cousins will return."

"Mother—"

"Any shame for not being married," Zipporah said firmly, "is borne by your eldest sister. Can't you bear it with her?"

"I hate her," Zenobia hissed. "I wish she were never born. There's nothing worse than an ugly, older sister. It's the curse of God!"

"Zenobia! You will be quiet!" Zipporah said sternly. "There was never a sweeter child born to parents in Israel than your sister.

I thank the Lord every day for having sent her to me. And I won't hear another word about it. You are going to the wedding and you are going to smile and bring blessings on our family. Now go and prepare. Immediately!"

Zenobia and Isis and their younger sisters all went to the wedding. The two eldest smiled during the celebration as their mother had directed, but they were sullen for days after. Isis cried constantly. Zenobia turned bitter as a green olive. Lemuel and Sam, previously not good enough for Zenobia and Isis, suddenly became handsome, witty, and altogether desirable now that they were missing.

Ishmael, unable to calm the female members of his family, at last agreed to make a trip to Jerusalem. "At least there I may find peace!" were his parting words. He planned to be gone several weeks, taking his sons Harun and Quarun and their families with him to stay in Jerusalem to settle Lehi's affairs.

After they left with Ishmael, Zenobia and Isis complained more than before. And when not under the stern gaze of Zipporah, they teased Yobina unmercifully. Their words, like fleas, bit and pinched. Ari'el was glad to escape her gloomy home each day and find peace alone with her lambs in the green pastures.

Aware of the pain in Yobina's heart, she offered to trade jobs so Yobina could escape the house. But Yobina refused, explaining gently that Ari'el was not skilled enough to do the family weaving yet.

"I could learn. I'd love to try," she said.

"I will remember your generous offer." Yobina hugged Ari'el. "It will comfort me. Silence is best, my little one. They can't argue with silence."'

"That's good advice," thought Ari'el. But *she* could never be silent in the face of injustice.

At last, Ishmael returned alone, leading a loaded donkey. He removed his large traveling hat and wiped the sweat from his face with the cloth Zipporah handed him.

"I left no stone unturned." Ishmael lowered his bushy eyebrows as his younger daughters giggled at his words. They suspected their father had delegated the job to his two capable sons but claimed credit for the deed for himself. They knew he was not a man of great ambition. Ishmael continued, "The servants were right. The entire family is gone. They left behind all their possessions except tents, camels, and provisions. Harun and Quarun are taking care of everything."

His words sobered his daughters.

"Everything left behind, you said?" Zipporah was stunned.

"Everything." Ishmael had been as surprised as his wife. "We searched his home in Jerusalem. We feel they must have left suddenly, to escape something or someone. They probably went to the south desert where fugitives hide from authority. I doubt they went to Egypt or Babylon. We'll know when they come back, when things settle down. Maybe then Lehi will come to his senses.

Zipporah replied sadly, "But with Lehi preaching against the influence of Egyptian corruption and telling everyone to submit to Babylon, everyone was calling him a subversive antinationalist. I've heard it said that Lehi's prophesying undermines the will of the soldiers who must fight for Judah's freedom."

Ishmael scratched his wiry beard. "The royal family is pressuring Zedekiah to rebel against Babylonian rule, to enlist the aid of Egypt. Not that I agree with them. Their idea of freedom would be freedom under the rule of Neco of Egypt, as it was before the war. Egyptian rule would be no freedom! Pah! It's more like freedom to promote Neco's popular debauchery!

"Lehi is right, but he shouldn't have spoken of it in public. It does no good. If only Lehi had stopped his prophesying!" Ishmael wagged his head.

"But Lehi only teaches what the prophet Jeremiah teaches!" Zipporah reminded her husband.

"Oh, yes." Ishmael looked at Zipporah. "Jeremiah is a good man, a brave man. But what reward does he have? Prison, Zipporah, prison. The king has locked him up and he wallows in the mud. The same would have happened to Lehi. At least Lehi did one smart thing—he left in time. I would have done the same if I walked in his shoes, but then I'm no prophet. The Jews up in Jerusalem will cry this and cry that. They will forever. Me, I'm content to sit under my own fig tree and grow old."

"But when will he come back, Ishmael? What about our daughters? And their betrothals? Our daughters can't bear much more, and frankly," Zipporah appealed to the father of her daughters, "neither can I."

Ishmael gave her no hope. "I don't know. Lehi himself can never come back. We will hope that his sons may. I'll have to think on it. Now, how about some supper? I'm a hungry man! Ah, what a good wife to have a pot of broth ready." After he ate, Ishmael would settle himself in the courtyard, and before too long the men of the village would come to learn his news.

Ari'el was glad in her heart that Uncle Lehi had said those things in Jerusalem even if he now was forced to run away and take his family with him. She would miss them all, terribly, horribly, achingly. Her heart felt empty. But she knew Uncle Lehi had done what was right. Deep inside, she knew he spoke the truth and she understood why Uncle Lehi had to spread the truth. Ari'el believed in speaking the truth even if her father didn't. The truth welled up inside her like a fountain and had to come out.

"I heard it all! You know my courtyard borders Ishmael's. I couldn't help it," Muriel eagerly told the others at the well. All the women set their large clay water pots on the ground and gave Muriel their full attention.

"It's about time Ishmael took a rod to those two girls. It serves them right!"

"The worst flirts I ever saw!" declared one.

Another spoke up. "I heard he now keeps them locked up."

"Yes, I haven't seen them out of the house since it happened."

"Those girls should have been married off years ago."

"The way they carried on with the soldiers! It isn't decent!"

The women nodded solemnly with Muriel, although one woman dared say, "At least they're not Babylonian soldiers."

"Acting like servants to the goddess Ashtoreth!" Muriel scoffed.

"Muriel! Don't say such a thing," said her neighbor.

"But it's true. Mark my words, if those two don't bear the shame of having babies but no husbands! From such behavior comes such things!"

The voices became quieter. "I hear talk that the new captain of the guard visits the women of the groves of Ashtoreth above Beersheba."

"Most soldiers do, as well as many other men," one woman said, shrugging off the captain's behavior until Muriel's sly hint followed.

"Maybe he won't have to anymore, eh? He's a fine catch and those two girls know it. They say he's fourth cousin to the king himself. Royalty. And here in Shilom!"

"I wonder why he wasn't taken to Babylon?"

"The clever and the very rich know how to escape."

"He's rich—richer than Lehi and more important than either Lehi or Ishmael."

"I wonder if the captain was sent here on Lehi's account?"

"But he's so young. This is his first post."

"He's ambitious."

"He's handsome."

"He's unmarried."

"Not for long."

"Hush! It's Ishmael's youngest coming. She fetches the water now."

The group was silent as Ari'el came toward them. Smiling slightly at the silent, staring women, Ari'el filled the water jar, then placed it on her head. To her alarm, the jar wobbled and began to slip, and she was forced to hold up her hands to balance it. If only she could carry water like Zenobia, she sighed to herself. Nobody could carry a water jar as well as Zenobia.

When the women thought Ari'el far enough away, they continued.

"She had the nerve to smile at us!"

"Disrespectful child!"

"Ishmael will have his hands full when that one comes of age. The other two will be nothing compared to her. Remember my words."

"Oh, come now! Ari'el is a good child."

"Can't even bake a decent loaf of bread!"

"Speaks her mind to anyone."

"To have five daughters. What a burden."

"Oh, the carryings on when it was heard that Lehi was gone. It sounded like a funeral the way those girls howled!" This from Ishmael's neighbor.

"I imagine the girls are near desperate."

"I'm glad I got my man before the war."

"They ought to marry off the eldest, if they can find someone who wants her."

"I'm glad my girls aren't homely," said one.

"And you can be thankful they aren't beautiful."

"And yours are?"

Not quite beyond hearing, Ari'el walked slowly, unused to carrying a full water jug. It kept tipping precariously from her head. So embarrassing! Carrying water was always Zenobia's job, but now Zenobia and Isis were confined to the house as punishment for flirting with the soldiers. Ishmael was adamant. Lotus was too fearful of the gossiping tongues to leave the house alone, so fetching the water had fallen to Ari'el. Even though she would rather be with her lambs, somebody had to fetch the water.

The family was in a shambles—Lehi gone, nobody to marry, her sisters in shame. If only some wonderful man would come and ask to marry Yobina. Any man! He didn't have to be rich or handsome, just someone who could discern how beautiful Yobina was on the inside so she would not have to suffer. Then Zenobia and Isis would find husbands soon enough and be done complaining.

Ari'el was so busy wishing that she almost tripped. Water splashed from the jar on her head onto her robe. She felt a firm hand on her arm steady her. In relief, Ari'el said, "Thank you for your kindness." Then she saw the captain's face.

"You almost fell," said the stranger, who Ari'el recognized immediately from her sisters' detailed descriptions. So this was the flirtatious captain. She looked at him curiously. His rich red robes were finer than even Cousin Laman's. Dark curling hair framed a swarthy face. His teeth were white against his skin, and his eyes were bold. Ari'el supposed he was handsome enough for those who liked bold young men.

And he looked familiar. Had she seen him in the marketplace? Ari'el tried to think where she might have seen him. Certainly not in Shilom? No, she remembered clearly: she had seen him in Jerusalem, among the men who had threatened Lehi. He was the young soldier, the one who had said she was pretty.

"Oh!" Ari'el gasped and hurried away.

The new captain stared after the young girl and laughed. "And who is that lovely young thing?" he asked his fellow soldier. "I've seen her."

"Too young. The youngest of Ishmael."

"The niece of Lehi?" the captain murmured to himself as he turned away thoughtfully. He knew he would see her again.

Chapter Six

Ari'el sat dreaming on the hillside of Mount Lehi, her dusty, sandaled feet sticking out in front of her like two brown pieces of wood. The once green grasses of spring had dried and sharpened, and they pricked her legs through her loose white robe. The late summer heat drifted up the high hill in waves. She felt like a toasted almond.

The gossip had at last calmed down. Zenobia and Isis were allowed once more to go out, and Ari'el was free to return to her lambs. Now that the growing lambs were bigger and stronger, she could lead them as far up the hill as Uncle Lehi's land.

This had always been Ari'el's favorite time of year, when she came with the lambs every day to visit her cousins. But this year was not the same. If she talked, she talked to the silent rocks. If she sang, it was lost to the wind. If she followed footsteps, it was only the footprints of mountain goats. The grapevines were unpruned, the olive trees sagged, the house was unlit and empty. There was no laughter, no teasing, no stories from Uncle Lehi.

Ari'el gazed over the lowlands and over the now dry wadi that began at her right and carved out the countryside. The land was brown, its monotony relieved only by the shadows hiding from the relentless sun. How fast the joy of spring had withered! She squinted her eyes and searched the stone-pocked landscape.

Her eyes settled on the large, smooth stone that covered the cave she had fallen into as a child when Nephi rescued her. A wave of nostalgia swept over her, a longing for those times when life was simple and fun. Now people were arguing, even in Shilom, talking of war and luxuries they yearned for that were hard to find. If Nephi were here, Ari'el thought wistfully, he would make everything fun again.

Watching the rock Ari'el squinted. Could the rock be moving? She stood up. It moved again. And again. She walked toward the cave, curiously, her lambs following. Something seemed to be coming out of her cave. And was that a staff lying on the ground? Cautiously, Ari'el took a few more steps, then stopped. Bags and more bags were popping out of the hole! And a mule was grazing on the hill nearby.

Suddenly, a head appeared, the face dark. Ari'el froze. How had anyone known about her cave, she wondered. Nervously, she looked up the hill to see how far away the shepherd boy was.

Then the rest of the stranger showed, and he turned and saw her. He wore the rough clothing of a tent dweller, woven from camel hair. There was no escaping now. But he grinned widely, his teeth gleaming in the sun. She dared to approach as he came toward her. Ari'el could scarcely believe her eyes. Could it be her Cousin Nephi? Was it only a mirage, a wave of hot sun born of her wishes? Without thinking, Ari'el flew over the dry ground and threw her thin brown arms around him. He felt solid and scratchy—real.

After only a brief moment, she felt Nephi pushing her away. Surprised and a little bewildered, Ari'el looked up at him and saw that beneath the dust, his face was as red as the tamarisk blossoms in spring. "Nephi, what is it?" she asked, her tears of joy and sniffles competing with her bewilderment at his cool welcome.

Nephi cleared his throat. "Ari'el, you mustn't go around hugging men. You're too big now for that sort of thing. You are no longer a child."

Now it was Ari'el's turn to blush. It was true. She had been changing underneath her robes this year. Her robes didn't hang on her the same way as they used to, but she didn't think anyone had noticed. She hung her head.

Nephi's face looked stricken. "I'm sorry if I hurt your feelings, little Ari'el. It's just . . . anyway, I think you're becoming very pretty. In fact, you're the prettiest girl I've seen for a while," he said with remarkable bravery.

His words brought the smile back to Ari'el's face and her tongue loosened. "Where have you been and why are you here? Why are you dressed like a tent dweller? What has happened to everyone? We've been so worried. Are you safe?"

"Not so many questions!" Nephi laughed and motioned for her to sit down on the rock beside the cave's entrance. "Yes, we're all safe. Laman, Lemuel, and Sam have come back with me, but they are at the house. We only came back to get something. Then we're going away again for good."

"Oh." Ari'el's smile rolled to the bottom of the hill.

"Look, can you keep a secret, Ari'el? Tell only your parents."

"Of course I can keep a secret! You know that. I never told that time Lemuel got caught tying the goat and lamb together and I've never ever told a living soul about this cave because you asked me not to. Speaking of this cave . . . you didn't tell me your family hid things here."

"You were too young to trust with such knowledge."

"How could you think such a thing! And I'm not young now! You can trust me completely."

"Then give me your oath."

Ari'el quickly stood up and said firmly, "As the Lord lives and as I live, I will never tell your secret except to my parents." She made a quick motion with her hands.

"Remember the old sheik my father loves to tell stories about? Our family is camped in the desert in Midian near the Red Sea, three days journey past the mines of Ezion-geber and under the sheik's protection. He is an old trading partner of my father's."

Nephi paused and searched Ari'el's face before he said, "Now the Lord has sent us back to get brass plates from Laban."

Ari'el didn't understand. "What do you mean?"

"Laban is the general of the army and he is over the garrison in Jerusalem. You wouldn't know about him. Anyway, he is the keeper of the records of our family—records that have been handed down by our forefathers. These records are vital because they contain the word of God and a genealogy of our fathers."

"Brass plates? But why do you want them now?"

"It is a commandment of the Lord."

"But why?"

"Because our descendants will need them."

"I still don't understand."

"Look Ari'el, we are going away to a land of promise and need the scriptures so that our descendants can know and learn the truth."

All Ari'el heard were the words *we are going away.* "Oh," she said quietly. "So when you get the plates you are going away?"

"Well, we don't have them yet. Laman asked Laban for them, and Laban threw him out, so now Laman wants to give up and go back to Father. But I think we can buy the plates from Laban." He waved to the bags lying on the ground. "If we trade him all of our riches it should be enough."

"Is that what is in these bags?"

"Yes."

"This Laban won't hurt you, will he?" Ari'el touched his sleeve.

Nephi looked up at Mount Lehi for a few moments. "The Lord will bless us. Father was told in a vision that we should get the records, so I'm sure the Lord will help us just as he helped our fathers cross the Red Sea.

Ari'el looked up at Nephi and a thrill went down her spine. Nephi turned away from the mount and looked down into Ari'el's face. "My father led us away because he saw a vision from God. We know that Jerusalem will soon be destroyed, Ari'el. After Father prophesied in Jerusalem, he was warned in another vision that the Jews there would try to kill him. He was promised a new home for his descendants—a fruitful and beautiful land."

Nephi paused, but when Ari'el said nothing, he continued. "The Jews think he is a fool for saying the strong walls of Jerusalem will fall. But Ari'el, I prayed to the Lord and I believe my father. The Lord has softened my heart. The Lord is very real." Nephi earnestly took both of Ari'el's hands in his. "He is just waiting for all of us to call upon him—all we have to do is ask and have faith and he will reveal his will. To anyone—anyone at all!" He hesitated, then asked, "Ari'el, do you believe in God?"

Ari'el quirked up one side of her mouth and one eyebrow. "Oh, Nephi, of course I believe in God. And I already know Uncle Lehi speaks the truth. I heard him speaking in Jerusalem the day before we came home. I saw you in the market and it was raining, but Lotus wouldn't let me come over to share your covering. Your father was hit with a rock just as we left. I believe everything I heard. I believe you too, Nephi, so you must do just as the Lord says. He may have a great purpose for you, just like he had for David and for Samuel."

Nephi dropped her hands and his jaw, staring at Ari'el as she spoke. She believed! Little Ari'el believed—little Ari'el who followed him around all his life like a lamb following its mother.

"The Lord will bless you, Nephi," Ari'el continued. Placing her hand on her chest, she said, "I feel it here. That's where I feel all these things. I know you will need great courage, but you can do anything with the Lord's help. Even defeat Laban's whole army, just like Gideon did."

Nephi felt humbled by the faith of his small cousin. "Thank you, Ari'el. I feel foolish. I thought I would need to teach you and instead, you've taught me. I need faith as strong as yours. Ari'el. Laman and Lemuel don't believe Father."

"I'm not surprised."

"If it weren't for Sam . . . " He picked up a pebble and threw it down the hill. "Sam believes our father and he believes me." He took a deep breath and said deliberately, "Ari'el, I heard the voice of God." He watched her face. "I know now for myself."

Ari'el's eyes grew wide. "Oh Nephi, I believe you. I wish I could go and help you! It all sounds so grand and glorious. I'm sure I could help."

"Not this time. This is real, not play, Ari'el." He looked away. "Very real. I thought it would be a fun adventure, but Laban is a powerful man." He clenched his hands. "My heart will not be afraid of him! My mind will not doubt the strength of God. We will buy the plates, if it takes all our wealth. I am not afraid to talk to Laban," he said with fierce control.

In wonder, Ari'el watched her cousin commit himself. So his bravery came from God! "You must stay with your family," Nephi said. He looked at her seriously. "I don't know if I'll ever see you again in this life, Ari'el, so never stop praying. If you keep the faith, the Lord will watch over you, no matter what happens to Jerusalem."

Tears slipped down Ari'el's cheeks unheeded. She bit her lip and blinked. "I will, Nephi. I'll pray. Are you sure I can't come?" How could she bear it, never to see her cousins again, especially this one? She admired Nephi more than anyone she knew. He had always been a bulwark to her and a staff to lean on.

"I'm sure. Good-bye, little cousin—or rather, my not-so-little cousin—and thanks."

"Good-bye, Nephi." The cousins held hands tightly for a brief moment before Nephi turned away. Ari'el saw that he was near tears as well. She watched him carry the heavy bags away and load them onto the donkey.

Ari'el ran after him. "Do you think the Lord will ever command you to come back and get me?"

Nephi smiled. "If he does, I promise I'll come. Here, take this little bag and give it to my sisters, Amber and Almira, as a present from their mother. She would want that. It's her own jewelry."

Ari'el gasped. "Aunt Sariah's jewels?"

Nephi nodded.

"But Nephi, they've been in her family for generations. They're precious."

"She has no need of them now."

"But your sisters might be in Jerusalem."

"Then save the jewels for them until they get back."

"I will. Good-bye, Nephi."

Nephi looked around at his father's land. Home. Then he turned back to Ari'el. She saw that tears were now streaming freely down Nephi's face. "Good-bye, little cousin," he said. "May the Lord bless you." And then he was gone.

Chapter Seven

Ari'el knew her name meant "Lioness of God, one who is brave," but at times it was harder to be brave than at other times. How much easier it would be to go with Nephi, to fight the whole army of Laban! How much easier it would be to face the deserts of Midian, to travel far distances to his land of promise! But to stay at home, to endure the complaints of Zenobia and Isis, to do the same boring things, day after day—to learn to bake bread, wash clothes, fetch water. That took bravery. To see loved ones leave and go far away took bravery. To say good-bye to Nephi took bravery.

Ari'el had to be brave now, truly brave, as brave as a lioness. As brave as Nephi tried to be, as brave as he wanted her to be.

After watching Nephi lead the donkey away, Ari'el led her small flock back through the town gates. As she passed the copper seller's booth, she stopped and peered into the flat, polished surface of the bottom of a kettle. "So Nephi thinks I'm pretty?" she whispered. She turned her face to see it at all angles and removed her veil. Maybe he was right, she might turn out pretty. She wriggled her eyebrows, then stuck out her tongue.

"Like what you see?" a strange, masculine voice asked.

Ari'el turned to see the new captain smiling at her. His white teeth glistened. She clutched Nephi's bag tightly to her and quickly walked away, the lambs following obediently. "He is nothing like Nephi," she thought.

When she arrived home, Zenobia's eyes fastened themselves on the bag in her hand. "What's that?"

Ari'el was too excited with her news to answer directly. "You'll never guess. I saw Cousin Nephi!"

Her sisters dropped their work and stared at her.

Ari'el continued. "Where are Father and Mother? I have to tell them."

"You saw Cousin Nephi?" Zenobia asked.

"We're saved!" Isis cried. Lotus trembled.

Ari'el began. "It really was such a coincidence. The Lord must have planned it. Today, I followed the shepherd up to Uncle Lehi's land. I was sitting there when I happened to see something move. It was Nephi. So I ran over and talked to him!"

"They've returned?" Zenobia demanded.

"Only to get something, then they are going away for good."

Zenobia came closer. "Going away for good? Where are they going? And what about our betrothals?"

"We . . . we didn't talk about marriage; we talked about God. I forgot to ask."

"You forgot!!" Zenobia whirled around. "You talked about God, hah! How stupid can you get?" Then she turned toward Ari'el again, took hold of her shoulders, and started to shake her. "How could I have such a stupid little sister? Can't you think? How can anyone, anyone with even a little bit of intelligence, forget a thing like that?"

"Let her go, Zenobia," Yobina said calmly.

"She's a stupid little dog. I refuse to call her my sister!"

"That's enough. She didn't mean any harm," Yobina said.

"Well, she's done it," Zenobia scoffed and threw Ari'el away from her like a damp cloth. "Let me see that bag!"

Ari'el cried out, "It's for Amber and Almira. It's for Nephi's sisters."

Zenobia ignored her and opened the bag. She poured out its contents onto the floor and all five girls gasped. What riches! What fine jewels! For a moment, nothing was said.

"Oh, Zenobia, have you ever seen anything like them?" Isis whispered reverently.

Zenobia had already slipped on a bracelet and chain. Isis grabbed a handful of the treasure and joined her sister in adorning herself.

In vain, Ari'el pleaded with them to put the jewels back in the bag, but the situation was beyond her control. Even Lotus and Yobina had no effect on their sisters.

"Look at me! I must look like a queen," Isis gloated as she paraded around the courtyard.

"They are beautiful! Look, I have five jeweled bracelets on each arm," Zenobia laughed. "A golden diadem. If only our royal captain could see me now!"

Isis turned to her sister. "Zenobia, what an idea. What great fun! Let's go out and walk near the guardhouse dressed like this." The two sisters knew enough not to go inside the guardhouse after their last punishment, but surely they could walk past the guardhouse, couldn't they?

"You can't go out like that! The jewels aren't yours, and Father will be angry." Ari'el could not stand back and let her sisters leave with the jewels.

Zenobia put on the last ring and said, "Amber and Almira will never know. Our father is too slow to get us husbands so we have to do it ourselves. There's nothing evil in wanting a husband and babies. Even old Uncle Lehi would approve of that." She smoothed her robes and adjusted her jewels. "If the captain sees our wealth, he may be encouraged to approach Father, and he's of high enough rank to please Father. Come, Isis, let's go quickly before the sun goes down."

"No, no, Isis, no Zenobia!" Ari'el ran after them and tried to pull them back, but Zenobia turned around and slapped her sharply across the face. Ari'el fell backward, and her two older sisters disappeared around the corner.

By the time Ari'el caught up, Zenobia and Isis were already in the marketplace, flaunting the jewels. The captain and his men watched appreciatively from the guardhouse door. Ari'el ran forward.

"You must not be here," she said to her sisters. "You must come home now." Her cheek was still red and starting to swell from Zenobia's blow. Her elbow ached where she had fallen on it, but she didn't care.

The soldiers were watching. The women were watching, wagging their heads. The old men were watching from the bench.

"Don't mind her, she's just our little maid," Isis lied to the guards.

Ari'el's eyes flashed. "I'm your *sister*, remember? Those are Aunt Sariah's jewels and they don't belong to you. If you lose one piece, you'll be in more trouble . . . "

"Don't pay any attention to her, she's just a child," said Zenobia. She stepped closer to Ari'el and pinched her arm. "Little fool," she whispered in Ari'el's ear.

"You're the fool, Zenobia. There's Father!"

She spoke truly, for there stood Ishmael near the guardhouse, not twenty feel away. He too was watching them.

Isis chose that moment to faint.

Later, Lotus whispered across the darkness, "I've never seen Father so angry."

"I told Zenobia and Isis he would be, but they wouldn't listen." Ari'el turned over onto her back and gazed up at the stars. Because of the heat, the girls were sleeping on the part of the roof where a temporary shelter or booth had been set up.

"Do you think Father will beat them?" Lotus asked.

The stars gazed back at Ari'el for a moment. "I don't think so. He's more angry than that. They've been closed in that hot room for a long time."

"I know. At least the neighbors won't hear this time. But we can't hear either. I wonder what he's saying to them. Mother went in a while ago."

"I wonder what they're doing?"

The two girls sat up and hung their chins over the parapet as the door to the closed room opened. Zipporah came out with her hands full of shining hair. The two erring girls' robes were draped over her arm. She was crying.

Lotus turned to her sister. "He's cut off their hair!"

"They'll have to wear sackcloth!"

"Can you imagine Isis and Zenobia looking like that?" The two girls covered their mouths and giggled. "Now they'll *have* to stay home."

"Quiet, girls!" Zipporah called.

Lotus lay down again under the twinkling stars, and soon Ari'el joined her sister. It had been an eventful day . . . seeing Nephi, the pain of parting, her worry over his safety, Zenobia and Isis, her mother placing a cool cloth on her swollen face.

"Lotus," Ari'el whispered after a while. "Are you still awake?"

"Yes."

"Do you remember when we heard Uncle Lehi? He said Jerusalem will be destroyed."

"I didn't hear him say that."

"Nephi said he did."

"Did he really say they won't be back?" Lotus asked.

"They don't plan to return. Uncle Lehi is moving them to a beautiful place that God has promised him."

Lotus sighed. "That's good. Now I won't have to get married so soon."

"I wish I could marry Nephi," Ari'el whispered. "I wish I could go away with him." Lotus was too shocked to say anything.

"Ari'el!" her father's voice echoed in the darkness. "I want to talk with you."

"I'd better go. At least *I* didn't do anything wrong."

As Ari'el approached her father, she heard him say, "Bury the jewels, Zipporah." Then he turned toward her. "Ari'el, come in here where we can be alone."

Ari'el obeyed instantly.

"Tell me exactly what your Cousin Nephi said." His eyes were troubled.

"I can tell you if you swear not to tell anyone but Mother." Ishmael promised solemnly.

Ari'el told him all. About the jewels, the cave, the secret of Uncle Lehi's whereabouts, the brass plates, their plans to go away. She did not tell her father that Nephi had said she was pretty and grown-up.

Ishmael was silent, then he said, "It seems I must bestir myself. This cannot wait any longer. You are sure there was no mention of betrothal?"

Although the room was warm, Ari'el shivered. "I'm sorry Father. I didn't ask. I never thought of it."

"Don't cry. I wish all my daughters cared as little about marriage."

"I don't think the sons of Lehi mean to wed my sisters. When I asked if I could go along with Nephi, he said no, that he would never see me again."

"You asked if you could go with him?" Ishmael roared with laughter. "At least there is some humor in this dreadful situation!" He chuckled for a long time, his round stomach jiggling. "Did you think you could get the brass plates from Laban yourself?" he teased her.

"Of course not," Ari'el answered indignantly. "The Lord will do it."

Ishmael stopped laughing and looked in amazement at his youngest daughter.

Ari'el broke the silence. "What are you going to do, Father?"

"Go after them. Make them come back and marry those two foolish daughters of mine. Somebody has to. I cannot bear another moment of their foolishness. I'll give them and half I own to the first man that comes along, rich or poor, good or evil!"

"You're going to Jerusalem to find my cousins?"

"It seems I must."

"Can I go?"

"No!" he roared. "Go back to bed." He opened the door, shouting, "Zipporah!"

"Yes, Ishmael?" Zipporah came from the corner.

"Pack my things. I'm leaving in the morning!"

Chapter Eight

Ari'el knew her mother was anxious. Zenobia and Isis were under her feet all the time, sulking like two spoiled children. "Can't you be a bit more patient like your older sister and cooperate with us all a little. We are trying our best to get you married to your cousins," she would tell her daughters. But it was a sore trial of her faith in the will of God to have her nephews gone away at this crucial time.

The first few days, Zenobia and Isis had been humble wearing scratchy sackcloth and with their heads shorn. That is, until the day the captain came to the house inquiring for Ishmael. He acted very friendly and stayed and sat at meat while Ari'el's mother served him. He introduced himself as Rosh.

After he left, Zenobia and Isis said his name, "Rosh," over and over, wondering for what purpose he had come calling on their father. Ari'el thought he might have come to spy on them to find out about Uncle Lehi. She didn't trust him, remembering that he had been with those men in Jerusalem.

Honestly, Ari'el couldn't understand her sisters after that. First they worried that they were growing old. Then they worried that the captain would see more of the other girls in the town than he did them. Then they worried about why Rosh had come to see Father. Did he want to marry one of them? They forgot the reason Father went away. "Why can't Father hurry back?" they muttered. When Ari'el told them Father was trying his best to get them husbands, Zenobia said only, "Hah!"

In spite of her brave words, Ari'el too wondered why Father had been so long and whether Nephi had been successful in buying the plates and if he had returned to the wilderness.

After a time, Zipporah grew short-tempered with all her daughters, even Yobina, in her worry for her husband. He was gone longer than the week they had planned, and she was burdened with the responsibility of the field work.

Ari'el learned something shocking one day. Wearing a sparkling white veil—a new practice inspired by Nephi's compliments—she heard the news at the well. She stood horrified, with her empty jug balanced on her head, listening. Deeply enmeshed in gossip, the women chattered for several minutes. By the time they noticed Ari'el, she had heard enough to glean most of their harvest.

The women said the sons of Lehi had caused a war in Jerusalem. The iron merchant from Jerusalem had seen it with his own eyes and had told the people of Shilom as he traveled through on his way to Beersheba. He said every available soldier was called out and every house was searched. The city was in an uproar for three days. But the sons of Lehi were nowhere to be found. They had disappeared like the morning dew. Ten people had been killed!

Ari'el dropped her jug and it shattered in the street. Twenty pairs of eyes fastened upon her.

The women expected her to speak, this child who was never at a loss for words. Surely she would say *something*. Ari'el was not known to be timid. The women watched her until she turned without a word and ran out of the market, past the guardhouse, and out the gate.

The old men and the soldiers watched. The captain gazed thoughtfully after her from his doorway. Clusters of workers who should have been at the harvest were deep in conversation, but they fell silent as Ari'el raced by as swiftly as a hunted roe before the arrow.

At last, outside the city walls and away from the crowds, Ari'el threw herself on the dry ground behind a large rock, where she could be hidden from all the eyes.

Was what the people were saying true? Or was it only gossip? It couldn't be true—but the iron merchant had been there and had seen it.

No one in Shilom knew better than she how true it could be. Hadn't Laban, general of the army, chased Laman away? And hadn't Nephi said he was going back to try again? Should she tell her mother the whole story when Father hadn't?

Father! All sorts of wild things went through her mind at the thought of her father—prison, house searches, torture. And her brothers' families were there in Jerusalem too. Ari'el's heart thumped against the hard, dry earth. No matter that her veil was dusty again—for Nephi was gone, gone forever. Perhaps he was a fugitive, or maybe even dead.

She had to calm her heart, to think with her head. She had to be brave or the whole town would suspect the truth. She would not tell.

Ari'el sat up and brushed most of the dust from her veil and cloak. She felt better. She was going to be sensible.

A trail of dust appeared on the road from the north—another messenger on a horse. She started back toward town for news, remembering how a messenger had come the day the captain visited their home.

Inside the gate, a crowd had gathered—wild for more news about the sons of Lehi. Quickly, like the Red Sea parted before the staff of Moses, the crowd parted for the messenger, who clambered into the gate and stopped at the guardhouse. Ari'el could see that he held an official scroll wrapped around a carved stick. It bore the mark of the king.

The crowd waited while the messenger went inside with Rosh. Ari'el stood quietly with them, her heart racing. At last the young captain came out and stood on the bench above them all. At the eager attention of the crowd, his chest swelled and his teeth flashed. A girl sighed. His eyes searched the crowd, stopped at Ari'el, and held her eyes. She kept her face still by willpower.

"General Laban was found dead on the streets of Jerusalem," Rosh announced. That was all.

At the house of Ishmael, six women waited. They waited anxiously, faithfully, prayerfully, fretfully, silently, complainingly, and hopelessly, according to their natures. They waited while they toiled, ate, and slept.

From beneath the shade of an olive tree, Ari'el waited as she watched her lambs. Now that she was older, she placed a mat under herself. She was determined to keep her veil and robes tidy. It was her way of expressing hope. If she ever saw Nephi again, she wanted to be clean. Older. Pretty. She knew it was only a dream . . . but Father had gone after them. Maybe someday . . .

Oh, it was no use hoping, everything was wrong. All her family could soon be imprisoned. Or dead! Jerusalem would probably be destroyed, and all of them with it.

She wished she could have gone with Nephi. In the shade of the olive tree, Ari'el began to enlarge on the dream she made up each afternoon. Imagine—imagine if Nephi came back and got them, and they could travel faraway. She would ride high on the back of a single-humped camel laden with tents and food. She would see ships, palaces, and great bazaars filled with fine silks and burning incense. She and Nephi would travel silently through danger at night, and camp by day beside an ever-flowing stream of water, or . . .

But no, these dreams were foolish. She didn't know where Nephi was or if Ishmael had found her cousins. She knew nothing. How could she expect to ride across deserts when she was always stuck here at home waiting. It wasn't fair that she had to be a girl.

A pebble hit her stomach. Ari'el sat up when another hit her arm. "Hey!" she said. She stood up and looked around her.

"Who is it?" she whispered toward the large rock that lay in the direction from which the pebbles came.

"Pssst," came from behind the rock.

A face peeked around the rock. It was the face of a young boy, younger than she, an unfamiliar face. He gestured to her to be quiet. "Are you Ari'el, daughter of Ishmael of Shilom?"

At Ari'el's nod, he continued. "I have a message for you."

Ari'el glanced over her shoulder toward the town, and as always, the landscape was bare of humanity. But just in case anyone should be watching, Ari'el walked casually toward the rock and sat down, as if nothing unusual were happening. But what an adventure! She could hardly sit still for the excitement. But she must.

The boy pulled a flat bone out of his breast and passed it to her.

"What is it?"

"Read it."

Ari'el read an Egyptian picture. "Lioness." Then came something that looked like an official seal, then the symbol of . . . death maybe? "Help. Bag. Trust. Beautiful Girl. Pray." Confusing!

"Who sent this?"

"He didn't say. The less I know the better."

"Was he young, a large, young man?" Was it Nephi perhaps?

"Yes, and he had dark hair. Desert dress."

Nephi! Ari'el's heart pounded like running horses. She read the message again. "Lioness of God." She knew that "Lioness" was herself, of course. But she didn't understand the next part of the picture. Since it was close to the Egyptian god of death, Ari'el wondered if perhaps it had something to do with Laban's death. Yes, an official! How did Nephi know? She suspected he had somehow been involved with that? Oh, no! Ari'el read on. "Help." He must have been involved. And now, he needed her help! She looked down at the rest of the picture. "Bag" was near "Help." That she could easily interpret but what did he mean—"bag" . . . bags! The day he was throwing bags of treasure. The bag he gave to her. They needed money to get out of the country. Of course! Nephi needed the jewels back. "Trust."

"Trust," she spoke aloud.

"You can trust me," said the boy.

"I will," she whispered.

The next part, "Beautiful Girl. Pray," was written in a tiny part of the corner. She fully understood that part and didn't say a word aloud, but her breath came in great gulps of excitement. Oh, she would help! She could finally do something instead of waiting like a blind cripple in the street. She could help Nephi. He asked for her help!

"I will have something to give you, but it is very precious. Can you take it safely?" she asked as she looked away from him.

"Yes," he whispered back. "Can you disguise it so it looks ordinary?"

"Yes. Where is he? Hiding?"

"I wasn't told where. I only know that my mother will be rewarded and so will I."

"You will. Thank you. This means a lot to me."

"I will be waiting outside the walls tonight behind the crumbled part where a repair has been made. I'll wait there all night. Be careful. No one must see us. I can't be followed."

"Tonight? In the dark? How can I?"

"You must find a way."

Her blood raced. Girls were never allowed out at night. Could she do it? "Are you hungry?" she asked.

His eyes answered her.

Minutes later, the messenger was eating the bread Ari'el had given him. While he ate, she quickly scratched a few answering words in Hebrew on the underside of the bone, hoping that Nephi could interpret her message as she had deciphered his. "The God of Egypt and of Israel delivers them that love and serve him. Likewise he delivers those who love and serve one another. They continue in prayer." Such a bold code, if he chose to interpret it that way!

In the afternoon, she tried to nap, though her body lay taut as a strung bow. Oh, to be able to do something at last! Nephi trusted her. And he called her beautiful girl. That's why she knew the message was from Nephi, the only person in the world that had called her pretty—well, besides Lotus. Did he mean it the same way Lotus did, simply to make her feel better? Or could it mean something special about her? Maybe when he read her message . . . Her toes tingled at the thought.

She was still tingling at sunset and again when the family was asleep. She said a prayer for the Lord's help. How she needed it! If only Father were home and could go out with her in the dark. Should she tell her mother? But Mother might forbid her to go. Her father hadn't told Mother about Nephi, so maybe she shouldn't either.

Ari'el already had an ink jar and a brush hidden in the storeroom prepared to paint a note, so she crept carefully over the sleeping forms of her sisters. All was quiet. Too quiet. She dug the treasure out of the ground in the corner of the courtyard, dusted it off, then glided into the storeroom to write a second, longer message that she'd been composing all afternoon. She planned to disguise the jewels as a marriage gift for a bride. Oh, she was clever! She was proud of herself. She remembered Zenobia's scathing words when she had forgotten to ask Nephi about the betrothals. This time she wouldn't forget.

Ari'el's hands were shaking so much that she accidently knocked the ink pot over and it shattered across the floor. The noise seemed to echo for hours. How could she be so stupid and clumsy? Her cousins would never be rescued now. Then she heard the noise of someone approaching. Ari'el sat as still as a dead body.

"Ari'el? Where are you?"

It was her mother. She opened the door.

"What are you doing in here?" her mother asked.

Ari'el made a quick decision. "Come in here, Mother, and I'll tell you. Close the door."

Ari'el swore her bewildered mother to secrecy, then poured out the whole story. It was such a relief to her soul!

"My poor baby! To carry such a burden alone. You should have told me about the brass plates and about Laban. And Laban—he is dead."

"I think the incident is connected."

"Ishmael should have told me before he left. Am I not to be trusted?"

"Perhaps he thought it wasn't important. How could he know what would happen?"

Zipporah was silent in the dimness as she considered the danger that Ishmael was in. Then she shook her thoughts away. "Well, now I know. I also know that Ishmael has not found them. What a good idea for you to retrieve the situation by sending a wedding gift! You're growing up, Ari'el. You must have thought hard about this."

Ari'el preened herself and said modestly, "I had all afternoon to come up with the idea."

"Light the large lamp, and I'll cover the window. We're going to do this right. Your words are good, but I can make it look more authentic." Zipporah went into action, as relieved as Ari'el was to have something to do at last. She proceeded to do a masterful job of disguising the jewels. She got out one of their last Egyptian parchments to write on, something Ari'el would not have dared do. Zipporah's note was a work of genius. She was able to communicate in grand language that four brothers were offering this marriage present to the four lovely daughters of Ishmael. Ari'el was amazed at her mother's ability to write so well.

"But mother, do you think we ought to have our name on the message?"

"It looks more authentic that way. And should something go wrong, we will find out so we can send further assistance."

"You know best," Ari'el agreed, but she didn't feel right about it inside. How would they know where Nephi was so they could help him if something went wrong?

"This ought to communicate very plainly what Ishmael's intentions are about betrothals."

Ari'el agreed. Indeed she was more personally interested in marriage than ever before. "Yes, it should."

"It is the last hope for my daughters."

"But my sisters must not know."

"That's true. However, someday we may be able to tell them how you tried to remedy your forgetfulness when you talked with Nephi."

"Oh, Mother, I'm so glad! Thank you so much for helping! I was scared to do it alone. I'm sure Nephi meant for Father to help me take care of this."

"I'm glad I woke up. Truly, it was a blessing that you dropped the jar of ink. See how God works? Someday your sisters will all be married. Now, how are we to give the message and the jewels to the boy?"

She hesitated. "I'm to meet him outside the wall this very night."

"You can't go out at night."

"I have to."

"Then I'm coming with you. Remove your cloak and put on this old brown one so you blend into the dark. How do you plan to make it through the gate unseen?"

"Sometimes the guards are drunk. But if they aren't, I know a way over the wall if you can lift me from the inside."

"A way over the wall? How can you get back inside?"

"Oh, I've seen the boys do it a score of times. Some rocks outside the wall stick out to form sort of a stairway. It's great sport!"

"Ari'el!" Even at such a time, Zipporah could despair over her daughter's boyish ways.

The moon hid behind a bank of clouds as two shadows stole silently through the town. A dog scavenging through the town garbage in the darkness growled at them. Ari'el took her mother's hand. Outside the walls another dog howled. Shivers ran down Ari'el's spine.

The town was asleep, silent except for the footsteps of the lone guard who stalked the narrow streets. They could hear him in the distance. They crept from shadow to shadow, silent as Midianites stealing into a town at night, slinking past the guard.

If the guard caught them, what reason could two females, unescorted, give for being out at night? And on such an errand? All would be lost.

But all was not lost. The Lord was with them.

With Zipporah's help, Ari'el vaulted the town wall. Slowly, she crept toward the agreed-upon meeting place, keeping against the shadows. She murmured a prayer of thanksgiving when she saw the boy behind the crumbled rocks.

"Here's some food my mother packed for you." Ari'el pulled bread, cheese, and dried meat out of her cloak. He slipped it into his own cloak. "And here is the package. If anyone stops you and searches it, you are to say you are delivering a wedding gift to our family. Don't tell anyone where the men are hiding or who they are!"

"I don't know."

"Good. Guard this with your life. The help it will bring to those who receive it will be of more value than the riches themselves. May God go with you," she whispered.

"You may trust me," he responded.

"How I wish I could go with you!" If her mother were not waiting for her inside the wall, perhaps Ari'el would have dared to go.

The messenger paused and looked at her as though she were a lunatic to even think of doing a thing like traveling alone with a young boy, then he crept away.

In the distance, a single guard on horseback was silhouetted against the barren landscape by the light of the moon. Could it be Rosh the captain? Ari'el wondered. She waited until the clouds passed over the moon before she hurried back to safety.

"It's done," she told her mother after she jumped down from the wall.

When they were safely in their own courtyard again, Zipporah said, "I've been feeling that perhaps I should not have put our name on the note. In my zeal to see my daughters married, I may not have acted with caution."

"What's done is done, Mother. The Lord will bless Nephi's family. They are on a sacred mission."

A strange feeling came over Ari'el, a feeling that all would be well, but was not well at the moment. Why? She thought of all that could go wrong. Maybe she was too bold in sending the bone message back with the boy. Maybe she should have kept to the purpose of the mission—to help them escape—and forgotten her personal desires. How foolish she was! What would Nephi think of her message? And if he didn't mean his message in a romantic way, how could she ever face him if she saw him again? And what if the bone message was discovered by someone else? She would die of embarrassment.

Her mother was saying something about leaving their problems in the hands of the Lord. "This evening has restored my faith. Perhaps my brother was right to leave and I should trust him."

"You believe him, Mother?"

"Yes, I do. Now, perhaps the Lord will protect my Ishmael as well."

Chapter Nine

Zipporah dropped her grinding stone. "Ishmael!" Overjoyed to see that her husband was home safe, she ran to him and hugged him and kissed his beard. Soon he was surrounded by the welcoming cries of six women.

"Ishmael, tell us the news!" Zipporah asked.

"Yes, tell us," the girls echoed.

"Jerusalem is a crazy place! I'm beginning to think my brother-in-law, Lehi, was right," Ishmael told them. He was smiling and frowning at the same time.

"But what happened?" Yobina asked.

"General Laban was found dead. You probably already know that." Ishmael looked at Ari'el and said pointedly. "His servant Zoram killed him. I'll spare you the details, but Zoram was said to have stolen some very precious family records written on metal plates that were worth a fortune.

"It happened the night of the same day that the sons of Lehi were pursued, so some people thought the two events were related. But no one found evidence to sustain their suspicions."

"What about the war?"

"And the ten people who were killed?"

"War? Ten people killed?" asked an astonished Ishmael. "There has been no war."

To correct his obvious lack of knowledge, six women relayed several weeks of gossip all at once. They told about the war that the iron merchant had reported—the war started by their four cousins.

"Quiet!" he roared. "I will not listen to this. Women! Why have I been cursed with women? I will state the facts one time only.

One time only will you hear me. Your four cousins went to Laban to buy something from him. Laban, being Laban, wanted a better deal and accused them of robbery. He called for his guard of fifty. Your cousins apparently escaped the guard but no one knows because they haven't been seen since.

"The next day at dawn Laban was found in a back street . . . " Ishmael cleared his throat and continued . . . "murdered. His head was laying in the gutter and he was wearing only his inner robe. Later it was found that his ceremonial sword, his sacred family records, and his most trusted servant had all vanished.

"Naturally, his successor as general thought the sons of Lehi did it. But no one could prove that. Lehi's wealth also helped disprove it."

The girls gasped.

"The treasure of the House of Lehi was found in Laban's home. His successor, being anxious to retain it, found it convenient to accuse the servant Zoram who supposedly was greatly provoked against Laban. Laban had many servants serving seven years to pay off debts and had a reputation for using foul means to ensure that his debtors were unable to pay. Zoram was one of those suspected of being wronged. Since Zoram was missing, he was conveniently convicted.

"Laban was killed while he was on some shady errand that several elders were anxious to conceal. Harun, Quarun, and I decided it was wise to come home to stay in Shilom until this all passes over. We decided to leave Lehi's business affairs—what's left of them—to settle another time."

In response to his youngest daughter's questioning face, Ishmael nodded and Ari'el breathed easier than she had for weeks. So Nephi had the plates. And if the jewels she had sent were safely in his hands, then all was well. Her cousins were out of the country. Later she would tell her father about sending the jewels to them.

A heavy knock at the gate interrupted their joyous reunion.

"What more can happen?" sighed Zipporah.

It was the captain. "So you're back, Ishmael. I came once before and found you gone. I've been watching for your return so I could talk with you. Did you have a good journey?"

Hiding his surprise, Ishmael welcomed the captain as kindly as he would an old friend. He clapped him on the back and apologized for the disorder caused by his return. As the captain also was Jewish, his hands and feet were washed, after which he was shown toward the place of honor on the roof and, with Ishmael, served refreshments of wine and bread.

This time Isis and Zenobia were permitted to be willing servants, their shorn tresses covered with handsome new veils, their feet tripping eagerly to please their handsome guest. Though their lips were silent, their eyes spoke their admiration eloquently. Ishmael bore the captain's obvious pleasure with difficulty.

"I would like a private word with you, Ishmael," Rosh spoke when they were filled.

The girls retreated down the outside stairway that led to the courtyard and entered the room below the roof where the two men were sitting. "What is Rosh saying?" Zenobia whispered.

"I can't hear," Isis whispered back.

Ari'el climbed on top of a sturdy ceramic jar and put her ear close to the ceiling. She too wanted to hear!

Through the rush-covered wooden beams, Ari'el could catch a few of their words. She heard her father describe the confusion in Jerusalem. "But, then, I'm sure in your position, you are aware of news from Jerusalem," he ended.

"Not always. But there are things one does find out, even in Shilom, that they do not know in Jerusalem," Rosh said smoothly. "While you were gone, some rather interesting things happened— amazing happenings for such a small place. I thought when I came here to the south that nothing of consequence would ever happen."

"Egyptians?"

There was silence for a moment. "No. I found this on my doorstep several days ago. Perhaps a dog left it during the night."

"A bone? You bring me a bone?"

"Examine it, Ishmael."

Ari'el fell off her jar. A dog found the bone! The boy must have dropped it.

"Let me have a turn," Zenobia exclaimed.

"No!" Ari'el pushed her away. "This is my spot." This time she wouldn't let Zenobia win.

"It is obviously written to your daughter, Ishmael." She heard the captain ask, "Of what significance is this?"

"I have no idea," Ishmael sounded truly bewildered.

The captain did not seem to believe him. "The name, 'Lioness,' is obviously your youngest daughter, Ari'el. This indicates the death of an official, which proves that someone you know was in part responsible for the death of—" here the captain paused. "Perhaps Laban?"

"But I've never seen this bone before," Ishmael insisted.

"But you *were* in Jerusalem at the time of Laban's death?"

"I didn't arrive in Jerusalem until the day after he was killed. I had nothing to do with it."

"Perhaps not," the captain paused deliberately, "but there are people who would pay for this piece of evidence."

"A message on a bone? It could be from anyone." Ari'el thought her father sounded less sure than he wanted the captain to believe him to be. "And it has been proven that Zoram, the servant of Laban, killed him."

Rosh was persistent. "There are many people who would find it interesting that two coded names are together. Turn it over and look at the name on the back. I believe one of your nephews bears the name of an Egyptian deity. The people named are obviously members of the same family—or perhaps merely lovers. Men I know in Jerusalem would also find it interesting to note the reference to the death of an official. And who but their own uncle would give the sons of Lehi assistance?"

Silence.

Ari'el blushed at the captain's reference to lovers. What would her father think? But she had no time to worry about that now, far greater things were at stake.

Ishmael sounded angry. "Are you blackmailing me, Captain?"

"Call me Rosh."

Ishmael paused, then said, "Rosh."

"Rather, let us call it a friendly trade. Concealing the bone for . . . a few of the jewels such as those your daughters wore into town? Merely a mutual exchange of—something of worth."

"You insult my hospitality!" The ceiling above Ari'el shook as Ishmael stood up suddenly.

Rosh stood up also, more slowly. "If I were to show this bone to the right person, I would be promoted and would no doubt return to Jerusalem. But my tastes have grown simple now that I have come to Shilom. I like my independence here, where no superiors look over my shoulder." Ari'el shuddered at his cold and calculating tone. And he was really such a very young man to be so worldly. "I could be very comfortable possessing several fine jewels, Ishmael."

The captain waited until Ishmael sat down again in silence, then joined him.

"Oh no!" Ari'el couldn't help exclaiming.

"What are they saying? What? What?" Isis whispered loudly.

"Here, let me listen!" Zenobia pushed Ari'el off the jar.

"He wants some jewels from Father," Ari'el said in a low, desperate voice.

"The jewels? Aunt Sariah's jewels?"

"Yes! Zenobia, tell Mother we have to do something, quickly. They are gone and Father doesn't know. The captain must not find out!"

"What do you mean we don't have the jewels?" Zenobia looked fiercely angry.

"I'll explain later. Just tell Mother! What can we do? We must warn Father, but what else do we have to offer when trade has suffered so?"

"Land? Sheep?" Isis questioned.

Zenobia's eyes gleamed suddenly in the dim light of the olive oil lamp. "Isis, our father has beautiful daughters! Rosh can marry me," she cried.

Isis was quick to agree. "Or me! Go up and tell them now. Forget Mother. Hurry!"

Ari'el looked in horror at her sister. "Oh, Zenobia, to marry a man who would threaten our father, even if he is handsome and royalty? Think!" Ari'el cried.

"I'm thinking, I'm thinking," Zenobia smiled as she took a pitcher of wine to the roof. Seconds later, Isis grabbed a platter of bread and followed. "I'm going too."

"Isis," Ari'el cried in vain, embarrassed for them both. Then she resumed her place on the jar and listened intently.

Zenobia spoke first. "I understand that you seek a treasure from the house of Ishmael, Captain?"

"That I do." A pause, then his appreciative, "Thank you." Zenobia had no doubt poured him some wine.

"The House of Ishmael has greater treasures than jewels," Zenobia paused. Ari'el could hear more wine being poured. Oh, how to distract his interest away from the jewels? She grabbed a stick and poked it up through the rushes into Ishmael's thick robe. For several long moments, Ari'el heard nothing. Then the captain burst out laughing. "Do you know what your daughters are saying, Ishmael?"

"I do," Ishmael growled.

Zenobia continued smoothly, her confidence waxing stronger. "Our father is very rich with daughters. He would tell you that his daughters are the most precious of all his jewels. And he is more rich with daughters than with jewels."

Ari'el poked him again.

Ishmael chuckled. "Oh, that I am. I am! I have many daughters."

He'd gotten the idea. Ari'el began to breathe easier again.

"In fact," he continued, "you may have all *four* of my daughters as your price. Make me a poor man."

"A handsome offer," he said in a voice that made Ari'el squirm. "I might consider it . . . but you have five daughters."

"Yes. But I have only four daughters that are of age."

"And not spoken for?" he asked with an odd intensity.

"Not at all. You may have as many as you like."

The captain laughed, no doubt thoroughly pleased with himself, thought Ari'el. "It will be hard to choose. I think I will take only one for now. I am a poor man and cannot support more than one wife."

Ari'el heard her father stand quickly and say, "Here, I offer one daughter and a field." Ari'el knew that with his words he had offered his shoe from one foot.

"We have a deal," said the captain. Ari'el slid off her perch slowly. She could imagine what Zenobia and Isis were thinking.

"And where did this bone come from?" Ishmael demanded of Ari'el.

Ari'el knew just how Zenobia and Isis must have felt when their father cut their hair for he was staring at her in much the same way. She swallowed. "Mother can tell you about the boy that came with a message for help."

Ishmael looked at Zipporah. "She didn't tell me she sent the bone back with the boy, along with the package."

"I'm sorry. But how was I to know he would lose it?"

"If it *was* lost." Ishmael turned around and stared at the fire. "However, there is nothing we can do to find out about that. You say you didn't put their names on the note?"

"No, Ishmael, we did not."

"Good. I'm sure you did your best and Ari'el acted quickly tonight. For that I am thankful. Altogether it is not a bad situation. However, I will have no more of those kind of notes written from you, young lady!"

"You can't allow that *Philistine* to marry one of my daughters!" Zipporah exclaimed.

"I can and I will. Anyone who wants to marry one of the older ones can have them all!"

"Ishmael! But Sariah and I have planned."

Ari'el crept away while she could and crawled into bed, totally embarrassed about the bone message.

Chapter Ten

By the next evening, Ishmael was pleased with his cleverness. Two hits with one bold stroke! Judging from the way the captain had looked at Zenobia and Isis the night before, surely he would marry one or the other—and Ishmael meant for him to marry *both* of them. If the captain was really a poor man, as he said, Ishmael would throw in an extra field or two for their support. But first he had to find a husband for Yobina. He was sure the captain wouldn't select Yobina, and she must be betrothed first.

No one would need know of his nephew's involvement with the plates of Laban. While Ishmael realized that Lehi could never return safely, his sons might wish to. They were safe, God willing, and according to Ari'el, the Lord was willing.

Ishmael patted his satisfied belly in anticipation of the captain's visit. He had been in a tight spot last night, with a knot in his stomach as though he walked a narrow path between two deep pits. Ishmael had had a few bad moments, but he pulled through. How he had outsmarted that young fox!

The only thorn in his flesh was his wife's insistence that she had sent a reminder to his nephews of their duty. She wanted to wait for a response before committing any of her daughters to another man. Also, she was not pleased that any of her daughters would choose to marry a man who would blackmail his future father-in-law.

"Where will the blackmail end?" she had accused him after Ari'el had left. "No, my daughters are not for him. It is God's will that they marry the sons of my brother."

"Nonsense," Ishmael replied. He was the man of the family, and what he said was law. A bird in the sack was worth two in the tree. And the captain was clearly in his sack.

Zenobia and Isis were in heaven. They floated around like cherubim all day, for once speaking sweetly and patiently to all. To marry a man who was fourth cousin to the king, handsome and ambitious. How everyone would envy them! They worked to prepare for his arrival with unusual enthusiasm.

"Rosh is coming! How do I look?" Isis squealed.

"Shhh, don't let him hear you," Zenobia responded. "I'm so nervous."

"You, nervous?" Ari'el teased her. Zenobia was almost nice when she was happy.

Ishmael's other daughters were unaffected by the captain's impending visit. Yobina and Lotus had worked as usual. They felt little fear of being chosen by the captain, as did Ari'el. How glad she was that she was not yet thirteen years old. Thank goodness it wouldn't be her! Like Zipporah, Ari'el could not respect the character of a man who would blackmail his future father-in-law.

Despite her anguished feelings, Zipporah outdid herself with hospitality on the evening of the captain's visit. She realized that more than the honor of the House of Ishmael was at stake—indeed, her own brother's life was threatened, and the entire family was at risk. Harun and Quarun had joined their father for this important occasion, and Zipporah served a newly killed and roasted sheep, along with dates, almonds, and fresh fruit. Afterwards, the men by the fire in the courtyard rested and drank new wine.

"So, Rosh, have you made your choice?" Ishmael asked at last.

Zenobia held Isis' arm as they listened by the door.

"Don't squeeze so hard! I don't want to have a mark on me when we meet him," Isis hissed.

Rosh smiled silkily. "Almost. But of such an important decision, one must be certain," he deliberated. "May I see them dance?"

Ishmael wasn't happy with the request but dared not show his feelings. He clapped his hands and Zipporah appeared at his side. He spoke softly in her ear and she nodded.

Yobina came first and danced modestly while Zipporah beat a rhythm with a tambourine. The captain did not smile.

Zenobia and Isis came out together and did a dance much different from their eldest sister.

"Where did they learn such dancing?" growled Harun to Quarun.

Lotus came out and burst into tears. She was dismissed.

"Is that all?" the captain asked.

"Surely you don't want to see my youngest sister," said Harun. "She's only twelve."

"I'd like to see them all," Rosh stated, finally and emphatically.

Reluctantly, Ishmael clapped his hands again and Zipporah appeared. She went back inside.

"But Mother! Why should I go out? I'm only a child," Ari'el pleaded.

"You must. You know you must. Remember, he has the power to harm our family."

Ari'el closed her eyes. This was another way she must help Nephi. Maybe, she thought ironically, it was more exciting than waiting day after day. Still, she would rather have fought the wicked Laban than to dance for the captain.

The night was dark. The firelight flickered against the walls that surrounded the courtyard.

Ari'el approached her father and Rosh gracefully, bowing slightly. As she began to dance among the moving shadows, she moved modestly, perfectly. But despite her submissive posture, a rebellious flame shone in her eyes.

The captain smiled.

Deliberately, Ari'el refused to meet the captain's eyes. When she had finished, she rejoined her mother and sisters. "He is as bold as a starving wolf!" she proclaimed. "If I were a viper, I'd have bitten him!"

"Oh hush, Ari'el, he won't pick you anyway." Zenobia gave a satisfied purr.

The girls waited expectantly for their father. At last, Ishmael entered. Ari'el was surprised at how old her father looked. His weary eyes met her worried gaze.

"He has chosen Ari'el."

"Ari'el!" shrieked Zenobia and Isis. Yobina and Lotus looked equally stunned.

"Surely you are mistaken," Zipporah said.

"Unfortunately, there is no mistake," Harun said as he entered the room. Quarun followed.

"Me, Father? Why me?" Ari'el felt her heart had stopped in her throat.

Zenobia stomped an elegant sandal. "What does he see in Ari'el?"

"I don't know. We argued with him and used every reason there is, yet the more we argued, the more firm he became." Ishmael's voice grew softer and ended in a whimper. "Maybe he knew it would hurt me the most."

"But she is under age," Zipporah argued.

"He said he'd wait a year before their betrothal—for a bit of money," said Quarun bitterly.

"I should say so! How much money?"

"Enough," Ishmael sighed.

"We'll have to think of something," Harun said to Quarun. The eldest son, Harun had always been practical and responsible. He also liked his purse full. "We can't pay him all the money he wants. Business has been too bad this year."

Ari'el's thoughts raced. What about me? Doesn't anyone care about my life? How can they think only of money?

"There is nothing we can do." Ishmael looked at his wife, then back at his sons. "There are things you don't know."

Quarun was more philosophical. "Well, Father," he shrugged, "Rosh is a good catch and she may as well marry sooner than later. It's just as well he picked Ari'el since she has no cousin to marry. Mother's plan will prevail," he added.

Ishmael answered, almost persuaded, "He's certainly not the man I would have chosen for Ari'el, but . . . "

"There *are* advantages," Quarun stated.

Ari'el stared at her two brothers who had suddenly become strangers to her. She was shocked. Had growing up and doing men's business done this to them? She thought they loved her!

"Her four sisters must wed first!" Zipporah protested.

Ishmael sighed deeply. "He said I should be able to solve that problem."

"I just don't understand the man choosing a young girl," said Zipporah.

"It's because she's the prettiest. I always told her so," Lotus whispered.

Zenobia's eyes shot angry darts at Lotus.

Ari'el couldn't bear it any longer. "I don't want to marry him, Father. I don't! He's horrible! His hands are full of false gain. Please don't make me." Ari'el knelt sobbing on the ground before Ishmael.

"Horrible? Why, any girl in Shilom would marry him as fast as a wink. How many men like him come along?" Isis claimed.

Quarun agreed.

Zenobia could be silent no longer. Her words shot out like an angry snake. "The horrible thing is that he chose you, you foolish child! While I was locked in this hateful house, you were parading around the town before him! You should have been at home learning to bake bread this year. I hate you. I hate you!" She reached out quickly and pulled Ari'el's hair.

Ari'el yelped in pain. "Stop it! You can have him. You deserve each other. I'll give him to you!" In self-defense, she pushed Zenobia, who fell backward on a pile of mats. They glared at each other until Zipporah separated and scolded them. But oddly, the fight cleared the air between the two girls. They agreed on one thing—who should have Rosh.

"To bed, girls! Everyone to bed!" Zipporah commanded.

Ari'el pleaded, "Must I, Father? Must I marry him?"

"I gave my word. You gave your oath. Don't you remember?"

Ari'el swallowed. She remembered that she told Nephi, "As the Lord lives and as I live." As she lived. She pledged her very life, so lightly, never thinking—never thinking that she would be called upon to give it! Her whole life. How easily she had made that pledge, but how hard it would be to keep.

Even nature seemed to mock her as she lay prostrate mourning, unable to sleep, her face rubbed with ashes. The winds wailed through the courtyard, the birds hooted, the grasses on the roof rustled in twittery, mocking laughter. Footsteps echoed on the street outside as the guard passed by.

Perhaps it was even that awful captain, Ari'el thought. So what if he was good to look at and had those flashing white teeth that made the girls stare. So what if he was related to the king. His soul was a pit of mud and his heart was mean and cruel. He wanted to hurt Uncle Lehi. He wanted to hurt her father. He must want to hurt her also. Oh, why did he pick her? She was just a skinny, brown girl, and the one who least wanted to marry him. He must have known that. Why did he choose her? Why? Why?

She couldn't marry that man, live in his house, cook and clean for him every day, bear his children. The thought made her bones shake. All the gossip she heard about his visits to the groves. Why the man didn't even worship the true God, but Baal and Ashtoreth. True, he claimed to be a good Jew as many other people did, but Ari'el knew better. Didn't he do the very things Uncle Lehi taught against? Oh, to marry a man who was not a righteous man! Why couldn't he be like her cousin Nephi? If he were a man like Nephi, she would gladly follow him anywhere—anywhere!

Ari'el thought of Nephi, his brief note and his words "beautiful girl." Hot tears slid down her cheeks. Did Nephi ever think of her? Did he ever think of her as she thought of him since that note came? She wished it was Nephi she could marry someday. She would rather be the seventy and seventh wife of Nephi than the first wife of that captain. Gladly would she share Nephi with her sister Lotus. Gladly.

Nephi had so much faith. Faith! If Nephi could go before the mighty General Laban, couldn't she go before a mere captain? If she had enough faith, couldn't she persuade the captain not to marry her? If Nephi could be so brave, so could she.

She would go to Rosh tomorrow to persuade him to marry Zenobia instead. Even if it wasn't proper to go to him, it would be worth a try. Truly everyone would be happier, and surely her father would not be angry at her when her plan succeeded so well.

Satisfied with her plan, Ari'el soon fell asleep. Outside, the night wind wailed and the birds continued to hoot.

Chapter Eleven

Confident that she would receive her sister's eager cooperation, Ari'el went to Zenobia the next day. Ari'el needed her older sister's help to carry out her scheme.

"Do I look ugly enough?" she asked Zenobia as she dressed for her ordeal.

"We must not be too obvious," Zenobia said as she rubbed charcoal under Ari'el's eyes. "There, you look positively sickly!"

Now the next step. "You must smell terrible." Zenobia handed Ari'el a piece of folded clothing. "Here's a piece of Harun's sweaty clothing to tuck under your robe."

"Oh, thank you, Zenobia. I *am* unappealing, aren't I? What would I have done without your help? I know you were awfully mad at me last night, and I appreciate this all the more." Ari'el laughed, "At least we agree on one issue. He should marry you, not me. Zenobia, you must pray for me as you have never prayed before, with all your heart. I prayed so long last night that these shadows under my eyes are partly real. I'm scared."

"*You*, scared?" she said generously. She could afford to be generous now. "Never. That's another thing you and I have in common, we both have the nerve of a Philistine. You just stand up straight, march in there, and be as obnoxious as possible. That should be easy for you."

"Should I say thanks?" Ari'el smiled through her ash-whitened lips. "If I can make him detest me as much as I detest him, it'll be no problem!"

"Hurry before Mother sees us."

"Where is Father?"

"Killing a lamb for the winter, so he will be gone for a while."

Killing a lamb? Ari'el bit her lip, wiping off some of the white ash. She hated it when any of her lambs were killed. And right now she understood how a lamb must feel who was ready to be killed as a sacrificial offering. Nevertheless, she strengthened her resolve as she walked toward the guardhouse, whispering to herself.

"As Nephi went before the mighty Laban, I can go before this man. As Moses went before Pharaoh, I can go before this man. As David slew Goliath, surely I can defeat this man."

As she approached the door of the guardhouse where the soldiers stood gathered, she cried in her heart, "Oh Lord, help me!" The young captain stepped toward her.

"My little Ari'el, what a pleasant surprise!" Rosh greeted her, his famous white teeth flashing. All his men stared. "My future wife," he explained.

Ari'el bowed, then stood up. "I . . . I need to talk with you." Truly, she had never done anything so brave in all her life. She decided right then it was braver than waiting. Much braver!

"Come inside."

"Inside?"

"Are you afraid of me?"

She followed him. He closed the door.

"You can leave the door open," she squeaked.

The door stayed closed. The room seemed as dark as a cave. Ari'el began to shiver. Slowly her eyes adjusted to the dim light.

"Now, why did you come to talk to me?"

Ari'el's mind was blank. She had never before been alone with a strange man. She said the thought that had been on her mind ever since his visit the night before. "Why—why did you pick me?"

He laughed. "Don't you know?"

"No. I don't know."

"Come here." He opened a trunk and took out a mirror, with exotically carved designs on its handle—a mirror fit for a queen.

"It's lovely," she exclaimed. She glanced in the trunk to see if the bone was in there. If she could get it back . . .

"The other side is even more lovely. Come over by the light and look."

She glanced around at the contents of the room, but saw no bones.

"It's a mirror. Look at your reflection."

"Mine?" She saw a pale, worried face.

"It will look far better when the smudges are rubbed off from under your eyes." He took a cloth and tenderly rubbed her face.

Ari'el wondered, could it be that this man was kind and gentle? Where was the bold man she had known and feared?

"Now look," he commanded.

She looked again.

His voice was deep and comforting. "You see a budding flower. Not all can see the bloom yet, but in two years, it will be glorious. It has fire in it, but the wisdom to use it wisely. It is brave and stands up for what it feels is right, honors what it loves. If a man could own this bud, and the bud turned to the man as a bud turns to the sun, he would be truly rich."

Ari'el stared at him. Was he talking about her? Was she pretty and desirable to men? She looked into the mirror again. Was she really like a little flower? Her heart softened as she listened to his caressing words. Forgotten was the fearsome sound of his voice she had heard the night before. She smiled.

"See how beautiful you are and why I chose you of all the girls in Shilom? When we are married, you may have the mirror, to watch yourself bloom each day."

Mentioning marriage was the captain's mistake. Ari'el suddenly remembered why she had come and her heart hardened against him. "But I don't think I will make you happy. Truly you should choose Zenobia—or even Isis. Either of them would make you much happier than I would," she pleaded.

"Oh, no, my little flower," he laughed gently. "Their beauty will wilt. And truly they have thorns."

"Oh, but I have thorns too. You must believe me that I'm terrible! My thorns are much worse than my sisters'."

"Your sisters are like flowers fully bloomed. They show their bloom to everyone, and they will soon fade in so much light."

"No, no! They will only bloom for you, for all their lives. Truly!"

"Sit down here and tell me more." Rosh's gentleness disarmed her and she obeyed, anxious to persuade him. He sat down close to her. "I am like a honeybee hovering about the bud waiting for it to open," he spoke into her ear.

Ari'el decided it was time to speak plainly. She shifted slightly to increase the distance between them. "Captain, please marry my sisters instead of me. It would make us all happy, especially me."

His arm went around her shoulders. "This honeybee is hungry and would like a small foretaste." His chin touched her forehead, then he jerked away. "What is that abominable smell?" he asked.

"It's, it's . . . Oh, Captain, I don't like to be clean."

"Nonsense." He reached into her robe and pulled out the smelly garment.

At his touch, Ari'el screamed. Rosh, surprised at first, laughed and pulled her close to him, fiercely silencing her mouth with his.

Ari'el pushed him away and kicked against his legs.

"No one will interrupt us, so it serves no purpose to scream. Let me love you now—since you *will* be my wife someday." His arms were strong and determined despite Ari'el's sharp fingernails. Then her swift knee surprised him and he doubled over as she bolted out the door.

"Daughter of Belial!" he shouted. Gingerly, he sat down on a mat. "So she does have thorns," he muttered. But he wanted her all the more.

Ari'el didn't stop running until, safely within the walls of her home, she tucked herself behind the large pot in the storeroom.

"Ari'el, come out before Mother comes!" Zenobia pleaded.
She didn't move.

"Ari'el, what happened? Does he want to marry you or me?"

Ari'el was silent, her arms wrapped around her knees.

"Ari'el, what happened?" Zenobia actually knelt down beside her sister and put her hand on her shoulder in real concern. "Doesn't he want to marry me instead of you?"

"I'm never getting up again. My lips have been shamed," she whispered as she crouched on the ground with her head tucked into her knees.

"He kissed you? You let him?" Her eyes narrowed. "I thought . . ."

"Of course I didn't let him. He grabbed me."

"Well, you can't let anyone find out. If Father learns of this . . ."

Ari'el began to cry. "I don't want to marry him, but he still wants to marry me."

"He does? Ari'el, you must try again!"

"Never." She lifted her head. "I imagined I was like David before Goliath, but you have no idea how he can talk to a girl. . . . He showed me a beautiful mirror and told me I was a flower, and Zenobia, I started to believe him!"

Zenobia looked at Ari'el, her envy of her sister battling with her admiration for this man. "I knew he would be like that, so romantic and tender. I'm not giving up just like that. We've got to find a way to get him to change his mind. You don't want him and I do." Zenobia's eyes grew dreamy. "To be married to a man like him—a man so handsome and rich who speaks so sweetly—it would be heaven, pure heaven."

Ari'el felt older than her sister as she reminded her, "It would be heaven if he used those words only for you, but he must have spoken them many times before to many women. He was too good at it!"

Zenobia didn't seem to hear. "I'm going to try this time, Ari'el. I'll go to him. I'll make him speak those words to me, you'll see."

"I don't doubt you will, but he won't marry you. He says that you are a fully budded flower that has its petals open for all to see, but never to own for one's self."

"He said that about me?"

"Yes. Don't be a fool, Zenobia. He meant he didn't want you."

"Hah! You'll see!" And she was off to see the captain.

Ari'el stared at the empty space where her sister had been, then buried her face against her knees. What had happened? Didn't she have enough faith? She had been so sure she could persuade the captain. She thought she was strong. Was she so weak? For a moment she had even wanted to marry him! Oh, no! Oh, why hadn't the Lord helped her? Why?

Outside the guardhouse, Zenobia could hear her father's booming voice. "Zenobia! Come out of there at once!"

The door to the captain's room opened slowly. Zenobia came into the sunlight blinking. "Go home," Ishmael ordered.

The captain appeared.

"So you have changed your mind?" Ishmael asked.

"Oh, no, not a chance, though your daughter did her best to persuade me."

"You must marry her now." Ishmael motioned toward Zenobia.

The captain laughed. "I can assure you there is no need of that."

"The whole town will talk."

"Will they? I received another visit earlier today. Your youngest daughter also paid me a visit today. Now *that* was a visit worthy of gossip. I can even add to the tale."

Ishmael grew florid under his bushy beard. "Truly I shall have no virgins left in my house if I remain in Shilom!"

"You're surely not thinking of leaving, are you Ishmael?"

"We made an agreement, Captain, an agreement of lawful marriage. I will not permit my daughters to be ravaged or have any cause for them to be talked about!"

"Zenobia would never be ashamed," he said mockingly.

Ishmael ignored him. "I repeat, I will not allow my daughters to be shamed! If I have to, I will leave Shilom to keep them away from you. Have you no honor?"

"Very little," he chuckled. "I cannot promise to leave such exquisite flowers alone when they grow under my very door."

Ishmael looked with distaste at this man to whom he had promised his Ari'el. He said firmly, "At the Feast of Tabernacles, I shall take my daughters to Jerusalem where we will stay until Ari'el is thirteen years old. Not until then will we begin the betrothal. No sooner."

The captain was startled. He had not expected this. "Come now, Ishmael, be reasonable."

"I am their father!"

"Then a short betrothal . . . "

"A short betrothal, but nothing sooner."

"Very short."

Ishmael began to walk away.

"Ishmael?"

He stopped walking.

"I believe it may be a bit expensive for you to leave Shilom. I must have compensation for my sacrifice."

Ishmael waited.

"Twenty measures of silver a month?" the captain suggested.

"I am not a rich man."

"Then you will be poorer," he replied. He didn't look so hand-some at that moment. "I have many powerful relatives in Jerusalem who will be anxious about the welfare of my intended bride."

Ishmael turned away without a word.

Chapter

Twelve

At her family's house in Jeruselam, Ari'el climbed the stairs to the top of their home three times a day and knelt facing the temple. She sang the words of a psalm she had composed:

"Oh, Lord, deliver me.
Save me with the mighty power of thy holy hand.
Carry me forth as the wind drives the rain.
Cradle me as a mother nurtures her young one.
Nourish me as the rain falls gently upon new grasses.
Oh, save me Lord.
Deliver me from my trials,
End all my grief.
Bear me up and away from all trouble,
The darkness, the ever gaping hole.
It stretches open before me
Causing me to tremble
As dry grass shivers before the furnace.
Send thy healing rains,
And with thy loving tears, quench the fire.
End all my trials.
Deliver me.
Oh, Lord, save me."

"Why does she go up there?" Ishmael asked his wife.

"She sings."

"Sings? What does she sing?"

Zipporah responded rather proudly. "She composed a psalm." After a moment she added, "I worry constantly about her. Every day she looks more like a shadow. Is there nothing you can do for her?"

Ishmael fingered his graying beard. "I have a plan."

Zipporah waited.

"A daughter cannot marry or be betrothed before her older sisters. Yobina is a great blessing to us now in this difficult circumstance. There were few men who would wed her before and now there are even fewer in the city. And our nephews will not return to betroth them before Rosh comes. He will give up."

"That is your plan? That is all?" exclaimed Zipporah. "Will you keep paying the captain forever to wait for Ari'el while you delay? You expect a man like him to be patient? He will want her. Ishmael, beware . . . beware of that young man. You must have a better plan."

"Woman, have you no respect for me?" Ishmael was angry, for in truth, he had no better plan.

Zipporah was silent, then said, "I believe you can think of a better plan." Then she left him alone to ponder her words.

Ishmael watched Ari'el thoughtfully as she climbed down from the roof. "If I must sacrifice her, I must," he whispered. His eyes were bleak.

Ari'el went about her daily chores automatically, feeling humble and empty. When she walked to market, she no longer picked out certain stones or avoided blood on the street. The blood had been washed away by the tears of heaven.

Living in Jerusalem, one could not ignore its evils—such as the sacrifice of infants in the Valley of Himnon on fiery altars to the hungry god, Molek—one could only endure them. Ari'el dreamed of those flames and wished they would consume *her*.

She endured the tattered beggars, emptying her pockets until they were barren. She had no more to give. Would that the Babylonians would come and end all this! Would that she could be carried away as the upper classes were many months ago . . . away from this misery and away from the wicked captain. If she could never join her cousins, then Babylon would seem a paradise compared to her fate in this land. Surely, the iniquity within the walls of Jerusalem made them ripe to fall. Already the cracked walls were crumbling.

On the day she learned she was being followed, Ari'el went out the door with Lotus to shop at the market. They walked together, Ari'el's steps as sedate as her sister's. The marketplace was brim full of people. Like a shadow, she followed Lotus from stall to stall, bargaining with no heart. She was easily cheated.

"Ari'el, do you see the man in the blue turban?" Lotus whispered.

Ari'el looked around.

"Don't let him know you see him! He's behind that camel. He's here every day. He follows us."

Suddenly the blood in her veins rushed like water in the spring. "We must leave," she said with more life in her voice than Lotus had heard for months.

Lotus took her hand and they slipped behind the stall. Lotus gave silver to the seller for his silence.

The blue-turbaned man offered the seller more silver. He took it and gestured. The man followed in the direction the girls had disappeared.

Ari'el took the lead and the two sisters raced through the tiny streets, winding, twisting, turning. Footsteps followed in time with theirs.

"Here!" Ari'el pulled Lotus into an open gate. They leaned against an ancient crumbling wall, struggling to silence their heavy breathing. Footsteps came closer as Ari'el prayed.

"We should never have left the crowds," Lotus whispered.

Ari'el squeezed her hand.

They heard the footsteps hurry past, hesitating at the open gate. Dare they move? All of a sudden they noticed something lying in the center of the courtyard—something more fearful than the footsteps: a body, a dead corpse. Flies circled it while birds of prey, perched above in the darkness, waited their turn.

Lotus started to scream before Ari'el silenced her mouth with her hand. In one moment her sense of preservation had returned in full. Ari'el wanted to live! She wanted to escape! Her heart hammered and her stomach churned as her nose filled with the smell of death.

The footsteps returned. Lotus' eyes were fastened on the corpse. Her body shook against the wall as Ari'el held her still.

The steps hesitated and stopped.

Ari'el and Lotus leaned further into the shadows. The steps came through the open gate and stopped. Suddenly they retreated and hurried down the street.

"Quickly—back the way we came!" Ari'el commanded.

Ishmael was solemn when told about their frightening adventure. "Undoubtedly, the man who followed you is a servant or a relative of our friend the captain. From now on, no one will leave this house but me," he pronounced.

Chapter Thirteen

On her thirteenth birthday, Ari'el sang her psalm ten times and she sang it ten times each day thereafter. Three days after she became of age, Rosh knocked on the door of their house in Jerusalem. He wore a purple robe with many tassels. He was shown every hospitality.

"Welcome, Captain." Ishmael had been expecting him.

"I have come for Ari'el. She is of age now." Ari'el and her sisters listened from behind a curtain of painted linen.

"That she is," Ishmael responded.

"I would like you to fulfill our bargain. I assume your daughter is prepared?"

With all the faith she possessed, Ari'el began to sing her psalm softly to herself. Only God could deliver her now.

Ishmael cleared his throat. "The young are always in a hurry. Why hurry?"

"I have waited long enough, almost a year. A year is a long time."

"Ah, well, it seems you must wait a bit longer, Rosh. It would not be lawful to betroth the youngest daughter before the eldest."

Ari'el peeked through a slit in the curtain. The captain was still as handsome as ever. And odiously self-assured. Zenobia moaned.

The captain looked hard at Ishmael. "You have not found Yobina a husband?"

"These things take time."

"I have given you enough time, Ishmael. Surely in a city the size of Jerusalem, a rich man . . . " his voice rose.

"It is a hard task to find husbands for four daughters."

"You think you are an old fox, Ishmael, but this *young* fox is far too clever for you. Read this." He handed Ishmael a crumpled parchment note. "I didn't want to have to do this since you will be my family, but you have played me false, Ishmael. I have come to claim my own."

Ishmael slowly read the paper. It was the note Zipporah had written to accompany the bag of jewels they sent to Lehi's sons! "Where did you find this?" he asked.

"It was found on the person of a small boy, who was no doubt serving as a messenger. He had been robbed of your daughters' wedding gifts and left for dead."

Ishmael was speechless.

Ari'el almost fainted. Nephi never got the note! Where was he? So it wasn't that the boy had carelessly lost the bone, but that he was dead and the jewels had been stolen! But why did the captain have both the bone and the letter? And the jewels—did he also have the jewels? That dog story sounded mighty suspicious to her now. Or could a dog have taken the bone from the corpse of the boy? No wonder she had had a terrible feeling that night.

"The note proves that your daughters are betrothed, all four of them, as it says. Can you deny it?"

Ishmael thought quickly. "I suppose not." He dared not admit that there was any connection between the bone and the parchment note! Now his older daughters were supposedly already betrothed. Though the wedding message had no bridegroom names on it, there was no way out. Still, Ishmael tried again: "Since we didn't receive this we weren't sure . . ."

"Of course. I'm sorry to break the news of the loss of wedding presents in this way and after all this time, but surely the good news of the betrothal of four daughters at once will make up for my tardiness. I will not stay. For double our agreed payment, I will generously give you an extra week to make it up to you. My betrothal to Ari'el will begin one week from today. One week after that will be the wedding. I can wait no longer. That will give you time to prepare." Then he left.

"You should have asked for more time," Zipporah scolded. But when she saw his crestfallen expression, she refrained from adding that Ishmael's plan had failed completely.

"It doesn't matter," Ishmael said to his wife. "Better to have it over with." Putting ashes on his forehead, Ishmael lay on his mat, his face to the wall.

Ishmael remained on his mat all week, a stricken man. Zipporah stayed by his side. Yobina continued to weave, Lotus and Ari'el prepared the meals, and Zenobia and Isis made plans.

"Not that I don't respect Father," Zenobia said, "but now is not a time to be sick. We will never get husbands that way. Ari'el will be the only one among us to be married and have babies. And the rest of us? We will turn grey waiting for our tardy betrothed to come out of the desert. They may already have wives for all we know. They don't even know they are betrothed to us, and while we are considered betrothed, no other man will dare marry us, even me. I say we do something!"

"I agree," said Isis, jingling her bracelets.

"How can we?" asked Lotus.

"What can we do?" Yobina asked. She too was troubled.

"I have a plan," Zenobia told them. "Lotus has often said that Ari'el looks like me. I know she says it just to annoy me, but I'm admitting it at last. Now that Ari'el is older and nearly as tall as I am, she does resemble me, and that very fact is in our favor." All eight eyes followed every movement she made. She touched her hair, her bracelet, her girdle. "Ari'el doesn't want Rosh, but I do—so *I* shall be Ari'el."

"It's a marvelous idea!" Isis cried enthusiastically, always quick to support Zenobia.

"But how?" asked Lotus, more practically.

"Hush! Trade clothes with me, Ari'el. We must practice."

"Try it, Ari'el," Yobina urged. "It worked for Leah of ancient days."

Looking toward Yobina for confirmation, Ari'el began to remove her robe. Zenobia snatched it quickly and put it on.

"How do I look?" she asked, swirling and dipping.

"It'll never work," Ari'el wailed.

"What about that faith you always talk about," said Isis. "I see you praying all the time. Surely your God will blind the eyes of the captain."

"Stop smoothing the robe and touching yourself. Ari'el isn't vain like that," Yobina told Zenobia.

Zenobia's glance at Yobina would have burned dinner, but she held her hands still.

"Mess up your hair," said Lotus.

"I don't wear my hair messy!" Zenobia protested.

"That's how the captain has always seen Ari'el. Mess up your hair, Zenobia."

"Do I have to?" Zenobia protested.

"How much do you want to marry the captain?"

Zenobia messed up her hair.

Lotus rubbed the veil on the dirt floor and put it on Zenobia.

Zenobia's nose wrinkled. "How do I look?"

"Move your eyebrows," said Isis.

"Walk. No, glide. Ari'el is very graceful," said Lotus.

"She does look like Ari'el," Yobina gasped.

"No one will tell Father until it's done," Zenobia smirked. "The day of the betrothal, Lotus will take Ari'el out and I will be here. I will even smell a bit," she said, smiling.

Ari'el shuddered, remembering how the captain had reached inside her robe for her brother's sweaty garment. But Zenobia's confidence was infectious. "Are you sure you want to do this?" Her words breathed hope, escape.

"Very sure."

Above the city, the day was bright and clear. Zipporah was ready, her face set. Zenobia was dressed for Rosh. Ishmael stayed in bed.

Lotus and Ari'el slipped away from the house until after the day's events had been completed. Their mother wouldn't miss them until they were far away, and when she finally found out why they were missing—well, she would have to substitute Zenobia. The two girls hadn't been out for weeks and they felt as free as two children in the sun.

"Where shall we go?" Lotus asked. "We have to stay all day."

"First we will go to the temple and we will offer sacrifice. May our prayers be answered!" Ari'el's heart harbored a great fear that Zenobia's plan would not work—that she would return home to an unsmiling captain who would still be waiting for her.

"You've offered enough prayers for fifty answers," Lotus said.

Today, for a change, Ari'el kept her coins in her pockets, resolutely refusing the outstretched hands and pitiful cries of the beggars. Her money was for a burned sacrifice. A whole lamb.

The two girls cleansed themselves and entered the outer court of Solomon's temple. The smell of incense and burning meat was everywhere. They stopped and gazed about them.

A crowd of people had gathered in the corner to hear an old man who appeared to be prophesying in a loud voice. The people in the courtyard seemed to like his words. Ari'el beckoned Lotus to follow her toward him. But but when they came within the sound of his voice, Ari'el turned away. "He's no prophet," she whispered.

As Ari'el and Lotus turned away from the false prophet, their eyes fell upon a new statue of a woman with wings, which stood in the corner directly opposite them. It was Ashtoreth the consort of the god Baal. Several of her priestesses walked back and forth seductively under her wings until a man came forward and took one of them inside a private door behind the graven image.

Lotus was shocked. Ari'el felt sick.

"Come away," Lotus said as she took Ari'el's arm.

"I have to make a sacrifice and this is the only temple the Lord has!" She had come here to worship the true and living God, no matter how corrupted the temple had become. Her God was more powerful than gods of clay and stone. Surely he could send deliverance, even at this last hour!

She purchased an offering, then waited and watched as the animal was sacrificed. It was as if she had knelt down and placed her heart on the altar as a sacrifice.

"Oh, Ari'el!" Lotus put her arms around her and wept. "What if Zenobia's plan doesn't work?"

"It's all right. I feel peace at last."

For hours, the girls wandered solemnly through the streets of Jerusalem, past the beggars, shopkeepers, and trains of pack animals. When they entered the gate of their home, it was sunset.

Lotus caught Ari'el's arm and held her back. "Wait, they are still entertaining. Is the captain still here? Look, it's Father and he's smiling!" Hope sprang up in Ari'el's breast like a shoot of new spring wheat. When she saw Cousin Sam and Cousin Lemuel standing with her mother and father, Ari'el felt that her heart must burst with joy!

"Quickly girls, quickly," Zipporah whispered. "We must hurry! We are ready to leave with them. The Lord has told Lehi to send for us and you will all be married! All of you, for there is a man for Yobina. I never thought it would work out that way; I thought Laman would marry her, but this is good enough. The Lord's will is done! He has heard our prayers but we must leave at once."

Ari'el's feet stood rooted to the ground. "Do you mean we are leaving Jerusalem? Now? Zenobia will not marry the captain?"

Zipporah scolded, "Don't just stand there, hurry! Nephi and Laman are waiting for us outside the walls."

"Do you mean that I don't have to marry the captain either?" Ari'el asked hopefully.

Ishmael looked up from where he was writing a letter. "The old fox has outsmarted the young fox," he laughed like his old self.

"But what has happened? And where is Zenobia?"

"Don't ask questions, just be quick!" said Zipporah.

Ari'el got down on her knees right then and there. She thanked her God. Truly she felt as Isaac must have felt when Abraham found the ram in the thicket. Her thin body quivered with relief.

"Are you strong enough to walk so far, Father?" Ari'el asked as they passed out of Jerusalem through the city gate. She couldn't help but look over her shoulder. This escape was too easy. In fact, the whole thing was hard to believe. Was she dreaming?

"I've never felt better!" Ishmael was a new man, now that his problems with the captain were over and his wife was content that their daughters would soon marry. "It will be good to get out on the desert again. After a week like this past one, I shall be happy to never see a city again! Lehi was right when he said we must go back to our desert roots. The Babylonians can have this city!"

"But how can we leave? Won't the captain follow us?" said Ari'el.

"You ask that cousin of yours—Nephi." Then he leaned down and whispered into her ear, "He's a good boy. You keep your eye on him no matter what your mother says. I'm the one with the final say of who marries whom!"

Chapter Fourteen

The journey to the tent of her Uncle Lehi had begun. Stars dotted the black skies above them like the sands of the seas. Ari'el bumped along atop a tall camel, her face veiled against the dust of the train ahead of her. It was just like in her dreams of adventure! She was on her way. A loving God had answered her prayers in the best possible way. Nephi had rescued her as she dreamed all the time he would. How much better this answer was than Zenobia's plan!

She gazed ahead at Nephi on his camel and tapped her own camel with a long stick. Nephi was leading her away, leading them all away. Her father, and even Harun and Quarun, had agreed to go and leave everything behind. That in itself was a miracle! But the real miracle was that she was here with Nephi, not married to a wicked captain. She would never forget what the Lord did for her.

She was amazed at how it had happened—it all seemed so simple. Nephi had come and told Ishmael that the messenger boy had been followed and robbed by the *captain* and was left injured to bleed and die. So what Rosh had told them about a dog finding the bone wasn't true! And Rosh had all of Aunt Sariah's jewels. Ishmael had suspected this but had no proof. Nephi provided the evidence. The boy had been revived by kind strangers who had been passing by. His mother was anxious that the captain receive the proper punishment for his crime, and she had written the details of the crime in a letter to Ishmael. Ishmael had shown the letter to the captain, who would not threaten or blackmail Ishmael again. It was all over, like a quenched fire. They would never get the jewels from the captain, but that mattered little to Nephi. All along the captain had known

Ishmael didn't have jewels, but he was so greedy that he put pressure on them, knowing he could get other payment.

Aunt Sariah had been so glad to see her sons that she didn't care about any of their treasures, let alone her jewels. Nephi told her that it had been a mistake to try to escape that way anyway. "I have learned that it is not wise to trust in the arm of flesh. Twice I did so on that journey, first when I tried to buy the plates from Laban, which was a dismal failure, and second when I made a plan to rely on our riches to help us to the land of Midian. In both cases, the Lord had a better way and showed me how right it was to rely on him. Though we waited for a long, frightening time inside a cave, our prayers were answered by a believer of the prophets who came to our assistance with camels and supplies. He would take no exchange for his gift. The Lord is good and we must always trust him with *all* our souls."

Ari'el's journey was just beginning. She saw that Nephi looked at her with new eyes. When he had first seen her, she was still dressed as Zenobia for her trip to the temple with Lotus. That in itself was enough to convince him she was all grown up! When he saw her, Nephi, without his usual composure, stammered, stuttered, and finally fell as silent as Sam.

Zenobia had insisted that Ari'el return her clothes immediately. She had quickly discerned that Nephi was in charge of the party and, in his new leadership role, he could receive his father's birthright instead of Laman. Quickly forgotten was the time he pushed her out of the tamarisk tree and the times he had sided against her in Ari'el's defense. Forgotten was her mother's plan for her to marry Lemuel. Forgotten too were her kisses with Laman and the handsome captain. Now her eyes were on Nephi. He would be the man in power.

Of course Nephi was completely unaware of Zenobia. He was a darling, naive fool, thought Ari'el, and innocent in the ways of women. Ari'el sighed, for she knew she loved him.

After many miles, Nephi called a halt to rest the animals from the heat of the day. As the older travelers gathered to cool their throats and discuss their various aching muscles, the younger travelers began to set up the tents against the sun's heat, and Nephi and Sam fed the camels. Zenobia sidled up behind Nephi. The camels, gathered in half circles around Nephi and Sam, eyed her through their long lashes as she leaned seductively against Nephi's arm.

But Nephi didn't look at her.

"Nephi," she said in a low voice.

"Hum?" He pushed more thistles into the camel's mouth.

"You do that so well."

"Feed a camel?"

Zenobia looked at the pieces of vegetation glued all over his hands with glistening camel saliva. She rolled her eyes and tried again. Sam ignored her.

"You're very strong . . . so large for a young man."

Nephi smiled and Zenobia was encouraged. She edged closer.

"You know the desert so well."

"I've learned the hard way."

"I feel safe with you."

This time he looked at her and smiled again. He and Sam exchanged glances.

"I like following you."

"Thanks. I appreciate that. Not everyone does."

"I do."

But Nephi was beginning to look uncomfortable. So was Sam.

Zenobia edged closer still, slid her arm around his, and leaned against him. The delicate silver bracelets clinked softly on her wrist. She shook her hair under her veil. It had begun to grow long again and it tickled Nephi's arm.

He stood up. Zenobia stood up beside him and looked up into his eyes.

"Look, Zenobia . . . " he started.

Just then Laman came around the corner of the tent and stopped. Sam saw him first and cleared his throat.

Nephi looked up at Laman's jealous expression. "Laman is watching."

"Who's Laman?" Zenobia fluttered her dark eyelashes. That had worked on the captain.

Nephi stepped back, bringing up his dirty, saliva-covered hands as if to push her away. Zenobia both saw and smelled his hands and moved back quickly. The camels grunted for more thistles, but Nephi knew he had to say something to Zenobia first.

"You don't fit prophecy, Zenobia."

"Prophecy?"

"You belong with Laman or Lemuel and I must marry a righteous woman so that my children will prosper in the promised
land."

Zenobia's voice was no longer sweetly soft. "What are you
talking about?" she demanded. "Are you trying to tell me I'm not
good enough for you?"

"Why do you wear clothes like that? Why don't you keep the
commandments of the Lord?" Nephi asked.

"Hah!" Zenobia snorted. "You haven't changed a bit—still self-
righteous and stubborn as a donkey. I wouldn't marry you if you
came covered in gold and trailed it behind you as far as Egypt!
You think you're the *king* around here. Well, we'll see about that!"
She flounced off toward Laman, who glowered at Nephi.

Later, as Ari'el was helping to take down the tent, she saw
Nephi approaching her. She thought he seemed embarrassed and
hid a smile as she continued to pull out the tent pegs.

Nephi stood above her and cleared his throat. "We should get
pretty far tonight. The next well is twenty miles away. There are a
couple of other groups traveling this way."

"Are they friendly?"

"Well, safe at any rate."

After placing the pegs in a neat stack, Ari'el next began to roll up
a section of tent. She paused before she asked a question that had
been on her mind for a long time. "Nephi, did the Lord tell you to
come back for us?"

"He told Father."

Her heart was full but she had to try to say what she had been
wanting to say since the beginning of the trip. "Words can't express
my gratitude, Nephi." That's all she could say.

"I know." He said no more either, but Ari'el knew he understood—about the lamb she sacrificed in the temple, about her willingness to keep her promise, about everything. Somehow Nephi
knew her heart.

Ari'el looked about her. How bright the night was! How clear
the outlines of the hills. Her spirit bubbled over with joy and she
laughed. She was happy again. Nephi laughed too.

After that whenever Nephi was near her they caught each others'
eyes and smiled. He had such a wonderful smile, Ari'el thought

happily. It made his whole being sparkle like sunshine on a mountain brook. Ari'el loved to make Nephi smile. And now his smile was different than when they were children. When they were young, his smiles for her were indulgent and affectionate, but now—they were approving and almost loving. Yes, loving! Maybe Nephi loved her. It made her tingle when he smiled at her.

Other smiles were being shyly tested as well—an entirely natural situation when five girls and four young men are thrown together. In light of the prospect of four upcoming marriages, the smiles grew quite openly inviting. Among the men, there was a lot of good-natured teasing; among the women, a lot of dreaming.

Ari'el, as one of the prettiest of Ishmael's daughters, received more than her share of the smiles, but Nephi's were the only ones she cared about. Lehi's sons were as newly enchanted with her maturity as if they had just been introduced to a completely captivating stranger.

However, Ari'el knew how to show young men that she was not so very interested in them. It made Ari'el laugh that the lordly Laman would look twice at her. However, she made sure he only looked twice. Lemuel only looked once before he was repulsed. Never would she marry one of them! She might as well have stayed in Jerusalem and married the captain.

Zenobia and Isis had seen the straying eyes of Laman and Lemuel and both were zealous in their efforts to keep as much male attention as possible on themselves. Isis wore all her jewelry and Zenobia went so far as to wet her lightweight linen robes so that they clung to her shapely body. However, when the cold wind blew the sand, her thin robes gave little protection and sand clung to every fold; soon she had replaced her thin garments with thicker robes like the rest of them wore.

Neither Yobina nor Lotus attempted to attract attention to themselves—especially Lotus, who was much too shy.

It seemed to Ari'el that Nephi saved his smiles only for her and she began to hope . . . to imagine what it would be like to be his wife. She loved the idea, though her mother was confused that *all* her matches going awry. Ishmael only laughed at her frustrations and all the young people's flirtations. The beginning of the journey was grand fun for everyone except Zipporah.

Chapter Fifteen

The journey grew hard. Gritty sand found its way into everyone's mouths and eyes and the food was bad. The girls were tired and sunburned. At night it was cold and they slept with fleas. They were thirsty, eternally thirsty—it was the way of the desert. They ought to have known that, living all their lives on its edge, but they didn't. Their throats were parched and stinging. Water became more precious than gold. Values changed, attitudes changed.

Laman seemed to have eyes only for Zenobia and no desire to marry Yobina. Yobina was actually relieved, especially when Nephi told her details about Zoram, Laban's former servant who awaited their arrival at the camp of Lehi. Since Zoram's escape with the sons of Lehi, he had become a free man and part of the family. Nephi spoke so well of him that Yobina thought such a potential husband much more to her liking than the arrogant Laman. Nephi assured her that Zoram was a fine man and a true friend. Before his enforced servitude, he had been a man of means and education. Nephi had told him of Yobina, and he had expressed his willingness to marry a woman of her humility and good works.

When the knowledge spread through the camp that Yobina might find a husband in Zoram and that Zenobia would be next to marry, she wasted no time reassuring Laman of her interest in him. Her smiles were now for him exclusively. Nephi was forgotten. After a few days, the mighty Laman followed her like a slave. Lemuel teased him, saying that he wanted to put a chain around his neck for a laugh.

Yes, Lemuel was the same joker. Isis alternated between scratching flea bites, giggling at Lemuel, and jingling her bracelets. If

Laman was Zenobia's slave, Lemuel was Isis' court jester. Isis was more than thrilled with the possibility of Lemuel for her husband. He was anxious to win Isis for his wife, and she showed every sign of being won.

But patience was wearing thin under this veneer of love and romance. The desert extracted its price of every soul who dared cross it. Each person who passed through was changed.

The desert seemed to magnify both virtues and vices in each of the travelers. Zenobia and Isis muttered even more often than they had in Shilom when they had no men at all. The only difference was that here Laman and Lemuel joined their chorus of laments.

Though she could sympathize with her sisters, Ari'el dared not complain. How could she murmur at her present lot? She had narrowly escaped a terrible fate by leaving Jerusalem. What were fleas and a dry tongue compared to freedom, stars, dreams? What did snakes and campfires and sore bones matter when she could ride behind Nephi? Though Nephi rode ahead of her, he was still present. She was no longer waiting in Jerusalem, nor was she in Shilom as wife of the unprincipled captain. She was with Nephi.

"H-Hello Ari'el," said Sam. He stood red to the ears with his first effort to talk to Ari'el after following her around in silence for the last three days.

"Hi, Sam. Nicer weather down here, like spring, except it doesn't look at all like spring." Not a hint of spring appeared in this desert wilderness. Its rocks had probably never seen a single blade of green grass since the earth's creation!

Sam stood silently watching Ari'el grind a few grains of wheat to make into bread to bake over the fire. Why didn't he talk, Ari'el thought impatiently. It wasn't as though she were a stranger or something. She was his cousin, a lifelong friend.

Finally, Ari'el said, "Was there something you wanted?"

Sam shifted his weight from one foot to the other and rubbed his robe nervously. Then he walked away.

Ari'el knew she shouldn't treat Sam so coldly, but he drove her crazy! What did he mean by watching her like this? She had so much work to do each day with the other women, setting up tents, cooking, and gathering fuel when they felt it was safe to light a fire. During the little bit of free time she had left, she wanted to sleep. It was hard work traveling in this barren land and riding on the lumpy top of a camel all night, a lot harder than keeping house in Shilom or in Jerusalem.

"Ari'el?" Lotus knelt beside her sister. "Did you just say something to hurt Sam's feelings?"

"Everything hurts Sam's feelings."

"You have to be more gentle with him, Ari'el."

"Why?"

"He wants to marry you, and he's trying to show it."

"Sam? Don't be ridiculous, why would he want to marry me?" Ari'el laughed. "Can you imagine how awful it would be? I'd eat him alive, I'm so much bolder than he is."

"Don't you notice the way he looks at you and stands by you?"

"How can I help but notice those two big feet?"

"Oh, Ari'el, be kind to him. He's so sweet, like a little boy."

Ari'el stopped her grinding and looked at Lotus. "*You* want to marry him, don't you, Lotus?"

Lotus blushed. "Mother wanted him to marry Isis of course, but Sam's the only man I'm not afraid of."

"I'll tell you a secret," Ari'el whispered. "I want you to marry him too. I won't be kind at all so I will break his heart, and he will turn to you for comfort." Ari'el laughed playfully, but Lotus was subdued and thoughtful. She had noticed that Ari'el laughed often these days.

But Ari'el's laughed less and less as the families toiled southward. She noticed that Nephi seldom came near her. And when he did speak to her, he was very stiff and formal. He no longer smiled at her in the special way he did at the beginning of the journey. What had she done wrong?

Once Nephi did talk with her and she thought he almost smiled, but then he walked away without a word when he saw Sam coming. Sam was so loyal to Nephi, a true brother. And Sam was so shy that he never expressed his feelings strongly. Nephi would never do anything to hurt Sam. Did he think Sam was interested in her? Was he afraid to hurt Sam's feelings? Oh dear! Would that keep Nephi from marrying her?

But Ari'el didn't want to marry Sam! And Lotus didn't want to marry Nephi—she loved Sam. Out of his loyalty to Sam, Nephi wanted Sam to marry the girl he loved. And Ari'el, out of loyalty to Lotus, wanted her to marry the man she loved. Most of all, Ari'el wanted to marry Nephi.

True, Nephi wasn't nearly as handsome as Cousin Laman, but who would want to marry a bossy man like Laman? He was always giving Nephi a hard time because Lehi had put Nephi in charge. Zenobia could have him. And who could stand Lemuel's jokes? Well, Isis seemed to like them. And then there was Sam. Ari'el sighed. What was she to do about Sam? This couldn't go on much longer.

The next time she saw Sam coming toward her, she got up and moved her work into the women's portion of the tent where he couldn't follow. As she left, she gave Lotus a little nudge on the shoulder. Ari'el prayed that Sam would notice Lotus and find courage to speak to her.

Still, Nephi avoided Ari'el. Ari'el saw that he often went on ahead to check the trail; at other times, he simply went off by himself when he wasn't busy. Each day the other men sat by the door of the tent planning or teasing the girls while they worked. Sometimes Ari'el felt like shaking Nephi. She wanted him to smile at her like he used to, or at least talk to her. Ari'el missed him, even more than she had in Jerusalem. Now she felt a different kind of separation, the even more painful separation of their hearts. Everyone appeared to be choosing a betrothed, everyone except Nephi. Maybe she had been imagining too much from his note and reading too much into his smiles. The thought saddened her.

By night the party traveled; by day they rested and slept in the safest place they could find that was near water. Day after day, they travelled the soft sands of the great wadi of the Araba Valley, one of the lowest in the world. Stars twinkled between the mountain peaks outlined in black as they rode through the nights.

Finally, Ari'el made a plan to talk to Nephi. Maybe she would be acting like Zenobia, but she had to do something.

But as the caravan came within sight of the well that morning, Laman pulled his camel to a halt. After the camel kneeled awkwardly in the sand, Laman dismounted, walked a few yards, and thrust his own staff into the ground. "We camp here," he declared.

As the leader, the choosing of the campsite was Nephi's responsibility. Everyone waited and watched. Although their camels paused, nobody climbed down.

Zenobia climbed off her camel, followed by Lemuel and Isis.

Nephi looked at them, touched his camel lightly with his stick, and continued on a short distance before he climbed down and planted his own staff into the sand.

Sam spurred his camel forward toward Nephi.

Ishmael spoke. "Get on your camel, Zenobia . . . Isis." But neither moved.

"Now!"

Slowly they remounted their camels. Although Ishmael moved forward to camp by Nephi, his two sons, Haran and Quaran, and their families remained with Laman.

As her sisters set up their tent under Ishmael's watchful eye, Ari'el slipped away. The dawn was cool, and Ari'el wrapped her cloak tightly around her as she followed Nephi. He stood at the well with the tired, thirsty beasts of burden.

"What are you doing here?" he asked sternly.

Ari'el squared her shoulders. "Following you as usual. Can I help?"

"Where's Sam?"

Ari'el looked at Nephi. "What do you mean, 'Where's Sam?'"

"Oh, I don't know. Never mind." He leaned over the well to pull the bag up. The camels leaned down to drink.

"It's terrible having the rest of the family camp over there," Ari'el said. "Is that what's been bothering you?"

Nephi looked at her, then away. "Isn't that enough?" he asked. "What can I do?"

"What does the Lord say?"

He looked at her, then bit his lip. The camels ran out of water and made horribly loud noises. Ari'el reached over and helped him draw more water from the well. They poured it into the stone trough together.

Nephi started to say something to her, but stopped. "At least Sam's behind me," he said instead.

"So's Father." She put her hand on his sleeve. "And so am I. What can I do to help you, Nephi?"

Nephi's answer surprised Ari'el. "Talk to Zenobia and Isis. Talk some sense into them. They want to go back to Jerusalem."

"I know."

"Zenobia wants Laman to be in charge."

"I know."

"I try. I try hard. Why won't they follow?" He looked like such a hurt little boy that she longed to reach over and hold him.

"Nephi, it's not you they won't follow. Of course it hurts their pride to be asked to follow a younger brother. But really, it's the Lord they won't follow."

He looked as if he was trying to understand her words.

"Who put you in charge?" she asked.

"Father. The Lord." He said softly, "I was warned they would rebel. But I was told that if I keep the commandments, I would be their ruler and teacher."

"Well? And have you kept the commandments? Have you been faithful?"

He stood up straight and answered, "Yes."

"It'll work out, you'll see." She smiled at him confidently.

Nephi found himself smiling back. Then he turned and looked at the mountains and said aloud, "I will *not* give up. My heart *will* take courage. My *mind* will be firm. My *soul* will be faithful. I *will* keep the commandments of my father!"

Ari'el stared, fascinated, watching the transformation in him. He seemed as if he could do anything in the world with the Lord's help.

After a few more moments he said, "You'd better go, Ari'el. Sam is by your tent." For a third time, he lowered the bag into the well.

"Sam is with Lotus," Ari'el said deliberately before she turned to go. Then she paused and said softly, "Nephi?"

When he looked up, she said, "Thanks for talking to me again," and walked quickly away.

Nephi stared at her back, rubbing his hand through his hair. He hadn't noticed that the trough was dry and the camels still thirsty until one of them spit, narrowly missing him. He continued his task thoughtfully.

Chapter Sixteen

After a very bad day of sleep for everyone, the girls woke up in the afternoon.

"Did you sleep well, Isis?" Ari'el asked her sister, who ignored her. Ari'el tried to be friendly. "Won't it be nice to get to the city of Ezion-geber tomorrow and see the ships and mines as well as the shops? What will you buy?"

"Who can sleep well when all you have under you is rocks." Isis pulled up her sleeve. "See, another bruise. It's the size of a pomegranate. I'm tired of sleeping in tents all day and sitting on a lumpy camel all night."

"But tomorrow we can go shopping in the markets. Won't that be wonderful?"

"It certainly will," Isis said shortly. "Even if it's not Jerusalem."

Zenobia woke up at the mention of Jerusalem. "I'm going back to Jerusalem," she boasted.

"How can you say that?" Ari'el said.

"There's a very good road that leads from Ezion-geber all the way back to Beersheba. Laman and I plan to be on it tomorrow. I've had enough of this desert life! I've eaten enough sand and scratched enough fleas to last me a lifetime."

"But Jerusalem will be destroyed. You can't go back."

"Who says?" Zenobia demanded.

Ari'el stood up to her. "Uncle Lehi . . . God!"

Zenobia scoffed. "Listen, Ari'el, Uncle Lehi's just a crazy old man with a lot of dreams. I've got Laman now and I'm ready to go home. And Laman wants his rightful inheritance."

"But Nephi says . . ."

"Nephi! That pompous little dog. Who ever heard of a younger brother that puts himself forward like he does? Why, I'd like see him try to put himself in charge of *me*."

"Oh, Zenobia, you have him all wrong. He didn't ask to be in charge—his father asked him to be. He doesn't like the responsibility at all. It hurts him when you won't follow him."

"Ha! You don't expect me to believe that, do you? I think he wants to lead us out into some forsaken wilderness and make himself a king."

"All Nephi wants to do is obey the Lord."

"But the covenant people live in Jerusalem, so why is Nephi dragging us through the desert?"

"Zenobia! Isis, talk some sense into her." She asked that before she realized how absurd her request was.

"I fully agree with Zenobia," Isis told her.

"You sound as though you like Nephi more than a little bit, Ari'el. Poor little Sam. He hangs after Lotus now. And Nephi ignores you. But I saw you chasing after him this morning." Zenobia poked Ari'el in the ribs.

"What do you mean?"

"First you were all set to marry Rosh and leave us out of it, and now that you think Nephi will have the birthright, you're after him. You think we haven't noticed?" said Zenobia scornfully.

"You know that's not true! You *know* I never wanted to marry the captain. I've always wanted Nephi, ever since I was a little girl, but I thought he was meant for Lotus." Ari'el added sorrowfully. "But now Nephi doesn't seem to want me."

Zenobia looked satisfied with Ari'el's last statement. "Well, I always wanted Laman and now I've got him fair and square. Even Mother accepts that now. And he's not going to be dominated by a bossy little brother. He's the firstborn, do you hear?"

"If he'd act better, his father would give him the birthright, but all he does is complain. Uncle Lehi has to put Nephi in charge because he's the only one who's obedient enough to lead!"

"Is that so? We'll see about that!" Zenobia marched out of the tent, leaving all the work to the rest of them.

"I'm sorry I made her angry," Ari'el said to Isis.

Isis only said, "It's not just her. Lemuel and I are going back to Jerusalem too, you know. Amber and Almira too. It's hard for them with the children. And Harun and Quarun were doing good business this year."

"But we lost so much to the captain."

"That won't happen again. You'll just have to face the fact that no one wants to follow Nephi to some promised land that probably doesn't exist." Isis walked away after Zenobia.

Zenobia and Isis never came back, so Yobina, Ari'el, and Lotus had to pack up by themselves that afternoon. It was dusk by the time they had finished. The camp seemed empty without the others. And Laman's camp still had the tents pitched. What was going on? Would they really decide to go back when they reached Ezion-geber? Father wouldn't allow it, and they'd have to follow Father.

Nephi and Sam were both away from camp. "Where's Sam?" Ari'el asked Lotus.

"Laman and Lemuel came over and sent him off to do something."

Ari'el stood up. A chill went through her bones. Where was Nephi? Something felt wrong, very wrong. "May I walk over toward the other camp, Mother?"

"All right. But be careful what you say."

"I will." Ari'el heard shouting from the side of the mountain. She ran back to camp.

"Mother, what is it?"

"I don't know. We must hurry!"

Ari'el ran, followed by Lotus and Zipporah. Oh what if they were in a fight? Someone was yelling and Laman had such a temper. Ever since he was a boy he'd had a terrible temper. He might do something awful . . . to Nephi! Ari'el ran faster.

Skirting a big rock she came upon Laman and Lemuel. They had tied up and gagged Nephi. Laman and Lemuel blocked her way.

"If you like the desert so much, you can stay here," Laman was saying.

Lemuel added something about leaving Nephi to wild animals, and the two brothers laughed.

Zipporah took one look at Nephi and told Lotus, "Hurry, run and get your father, he'll know what to do." Lotus ran back toward the camp.

"Oh, Nephi!" Ari'el cried. He looked at her, then closed his eyes. Laman and Lemuel began to walk away.

Lemuel grabbed her shoulder forcefully. "You stay away from him. Don't try to untie him, Ari'el, because you won't be able to."

Then it happened. Nephi struggled to stand and the thick ropes burst off his arms and legs as though they were no stronger than bread dough. Nephi looked surprised at the sudden answer to his prayer.

Suddenly, Zenobia and Isis arrived.

"Well, what did he decide?" Zenobia demanded of Laman.

"Oh, we took care of him!" Laman bragged. He waved toward Nephi, then saw him rubbing his sore arms. "How did you get loose?"

"It wasn't through my own power, but that of God, who gave me the strength."

"Can't you tie a better knot than that?" Zenobia mocked Laman and Lemuel.

Angry, the two brothers started toward Nephi again. "Why you little desert rat! You can't get away with that!" Laman raised his arm to strike Nephi.

"If you kill me, you will shed innocent blood and great condemnation will come upon you." Nephi stood unafraid. "Why can't you soften your hearts and accept the will of the Lord? You know he has led us by miraculous power out of a wicked land. We know that Jerusalem will be destroyed. Why do you want to go back and be destroyed with the wicked?"

"Innocent blood, hah! He wants to steal your birthright," Zenobia muttered. Zipporah looked at her eldest daughter sharply but for the moment said nothing.

Oh, where was Father? Ari'el thought desperately. And Sam? She couldn't let them kill her beloved Nephi. She promised to give all her life for his life once. Ari'el rushed forward as they pushed Nephi back on the ground with his arms pinned, one brother on each side.

"Stop it, stop it," she screamed. She grabbed Lemuel's arm and bit it. He didn't let go. Laman reached down to pick up a piece of broken rope. Ari'el kicked him hard in the side. Laman looked shocked and let go for a moment, which allowed Ari'el to quickly fling herself over Nephi's body. "If you tie him up, then you have to tie me up also. I will stay with Nephi to be eaten by wild animals."

At this, Zipporah stepped forward to speak but was interrupted by Sam, who arrived in time to hear Ari'el's words. Startled, he paused for a moment, then asked, "What is going on?" Lotus slipped to Sam's side as she arrived with the rest of the camp in tow, took his hand, and whispered quietly in his ear.

Baffled by Ari'el's defense of Nephi, Laman and Lemuel looked at each other as if to say "What do we do now?"

Zipporah could stay silent no longer. "Stop all this! Anger will get us nowhere. Bickering, complaining, fighting, like silly young children. It's time you grew up! Yes, you, Laman who are the first-born, just sit down there on the ground and listen."

Surprisingly, Laman sat.

"You, too, Zenobia and Isis. I'm ashamed to call you my daughters! I was ashamed when you went chasing after those soldiers back in Shilom. But I am more ashamed now."

Zenobia flinched at Laman's look. He hadn't heard about her escapades. Isis began to cry.

"Yes, a common hussy! Isis too. Then when the captain chose your sister, you were jealous. Oh, he's so handsome, so important. How dare you not love him? Don't think I didn't hear you twitting the poor girl. Gladly would she have traded places with you. But did the captain choose you? No, at least he had that much good sense, common robber though he was." Beneath Laman's hard gaze, Zenobia for once did not speak back to her mother.

Zipporah continued to rebuke her eldest daughter. "And now it seems that in spite of all my plans, the firstborn son of Lehi wants to marry you, right? But what kind of a wife will you make for a firstborn son? A complainer? A nag? The wife of a firstborn son should have dignity, should support him, and certainly should not encourage him to go against the wishes of his own father. No, you are not worthy of that honor. He would have fared better with your elder sister."

Zenobia looked stricken at the renewed possibility of Laman marrying Yobina.

"Isis, I feel no differently for you. I taught you both better than this. You must find it in your heart to remember the teachings of your parents. You must be as ashamed of your actions as I am.

"And you, Laman and Lemuel, the sons of my brother. What kind of sons are you? Do you bring honor to your father? Would a firstborn son behave as you have done today—trying to kill your own brother simply because he has tried to remind you of your duty to your father? A father who waits for you in his tent, ready to rejoice at your return with your brides-to-be?" She paused to look them all in the eyes one by one. "This should be a happy time, a time of rejoicing. But I am shamed for you."

Embarrassed, Laman and Lemuel lowered their eyes.

"My mother is right," said Harun. "It is utterly senseless to kill your brother. To disagree is one thing, but to kill him, that is another. I will have no part in it."

Zipporah looked in approval at her son's repentance and turned back to Laman and Lemuel. "Now rise up and be men! If you wish to lead, you must first be followers . . . of God, of your father, yes, and even of your younger brother since God has called him to lead us. It is time to stop your grumbling and complaining and be strong, stronger than this barren land. Strong, good, and pure as a stream of water, giving life, not death. If you will lead, then lead in righteousness and we will follow. The House of Ishmael follows the Lord. And Ishmael chooses to join Lehi in the desert." She looked at her husband, who had finally arrived and was standing speechless, quite amazed at the situation.

Zipporah was not finished. "My sons too will follow. They are familiar with the hardships of the desert and have enough wisdom to know you cannot return to Jerusalem in safety. There is no longer any justice there. You, Laman and Lemuel, have not lived there lately. You have not seen the Jews and how wicked they are becoming. Truly, they are ripe for destruction as your father says. You must live in a world of fantasy if you think you can return, for they will seek your life. And what will you have if you choose to go off on your own, without family? You are nothing but an outcast without family.

"Let us forgive one another and start again. Let us make this a time of rejoicing, of joy in the Lord who has given us our lives, our freedom, even the air we breathe. Let us all forgive one another. My sons must first ask forgiveness, my daughters as well. Then you, Laman, and you, Lemuel, must ask forgiveness of your brother Nephi for the wrong you have done to him, lest you become as Cain, forever wandering alone."

Zipporah looked at Zenobia and Isis sternly. Both were sobbing. As the eldest of Ishmael's sons, Harun went forward. "Cousin, can you forgive me?" He was followed by Quarun, then at Zipporah's bidding, her two daughters came and knelt before Nephi. They wept at his feet prettily.

Last of all, Laman and Lemuel approached Nephi, not meeting his eyes. "I'm sorry," mumbled Laman. Lemuel muttered something that sounded like, "Me too." Awkwardly they bowed down before Nephi. "We will follow where you lead us," Laman said, then he stood as if to walk away but Nephi grasped his arms and embraced him. Then he turned to Lemuel and embraced him as well.

"It is not me that you have wronged, but the Lord," Nephi told Laman and Lemuel gently. "It is to him that you must go to ask for forgiveness."

Ishmael spoke at last, his hands folded across his belly. "We all leave together when you are done with your prayers. See that they are long enough."

Without looking at anyone, Laman quickly walked away, followed by Lemuel.

Chapter Seventeen

While the others prayed, Ari'el ran up the mountain where she could be alone. She hid herself behind a rock and wept. Truly she would have died with Nephi; she would do anything for Nephi. She loved him dearly, more than her life! If they would have killed him. . . . It had been hard enough back in Jerusalem to give up her life to the captain so that Nephi might be free, but if Nephi had died . . . she would have perished too.

Even when she had been trapped by the captain, Ari'el had never been so frightened in all her life; she had never fought like that either. And to think her own family was the cause of it—her own sisters and cousins. Her body shook with huge jerks as she lay on the ground and wailed.

That was how Nephi found her. He knelt down and picked her up tenderly, as easily as if she were a baby. He held her on his lap much closer than he had so long ago when as a child he had found her crying in the cave.

It felt so good. Ari'el did not want to stop crying because Nephi might let her go. He continued to hold her until the moon rose over the mountain. She rested her head against his shoulder.

"I owe you my life," he whispered. "That was a very brave thing you did, but then you have always been brave. Why did you do it, Ari'el?"

She was silent for a while. "I had to," she whispered.

"Do you love Sam?"

She moved and immediately he stood up and set her on her feet. But she liked being held! It took courage to speak what she felt. She looked him in the eye. "No, Nephi, I don't love Sam other than as a cousin. He's very sweet and I don't want to hurt his feelings, but I *don't want to marry him*. I would make him a terrible wife. It's you . . . " she didn't know how to go on.

Nephi smiled. A burden seemed lifted from him. "I thought you felt that way when you fought for my life. Before that, I wasn't sure." He stood up straight and looked terribly serious. "Ari'el, before we left my father's tent, I told him that you were the daughter I wished to marry. He was very pleased and your father has given his approval."

Ari'el's heart filled with so much joy that her legs trembled. Then the evening stars seemed to shine more closely and she fainted with joy.

"Ari'el," Nephi cried. He caught her just before she fell. He gently laid her on the ground and watched her for a time. She was so beautiful and now he knew that someday she would be his. His heart swelled within him. He felt so very blessed. The Lord had prepared a mother for his children . . . and how righteous those children would be! Ari'el was all he could desire, valiant, loyal, a wife to follow him through all the trials of life, to stand at his side. He leaned over and softly placed his lips on her forehead.

Ari'el felt the soft wings of a butterfly touch her. She opened her eyes and saw Nephi's face so near. He had kissed her! She smiled softly.

"Do you love me, Ari'el?" he asked.

"You know I do, Nephi."

"You look so very beautiful lying there. Truly, as our father Jacob served fourteen years with joy for the love he had for our mother Rachel, so would I have been willing to serve thirty-five years for you."

"You wanted to marry me before?"

"Even if I had to marry all four of your sisters first!" They both thought of Zenobia, and Nephi added, laughing, "But I'm glad I don't have to!"

"Oh Nephi! When I think how unhappy we were apart! And I missed you so."

He touched her cheek. "The Lord has delivered you, and he will yet deliver us." He stood and helped her up. "Will you follow me wherever the Lord leads us?"

"Yes, Nephi."

He took her hand and together they walked toward the waiting caravan. "Tonight I will guide your camel," he said, smiling.

About the Author

Becky Paget,

As a young girl growing up in Pennsylvania, Becky had two loves—art and reading. But, as she entered Brigham Young University, the art department had the strongest attraction. She graduated with a Bachelors of Fine Arts in drawing and painting. Still, her interest in literature has never diminished. Finally, with stories of her own to tell, she started writing. She says, "My attitude was that if Nephi could build a ship, then I could write a book. We were both dependent on the help of the Lord."

Becky has pursued an interest in teaching art. She taught children's classes at the Contemporary Arts Museum in Houston, Texas, then developed a children's curriculum of "hands on" art history which she has taught in several locations. Becky currently works with the Laumier Sculpture Park in St. Louis.

Becky joined the Church of Jesus Christ of Latter-day Saints at the age of fifteen. She has served in many callings, and is currently serving as Stake Primary President. She lives in Webster Groves, Missouri with her husband Jon and their four children.